THE TIME MACHINE

H. G. WELLS, the th....................eeper, was born in Bromley in 1866. ....prenticeship in a draper's shop, he became a ....er at Midhurst Grammar School and won a scholarshi.. ..o study under T. H. Huxley at the Normal School of Science, South Kensington. He taught biology before becoming a professional writer and journalist. He wrote more than a hundred books, including novels, essays, histories and programmes for world regeneration.

Wells, who rose from obscurity to world fame, had an emotionally and intellectually turbulent life. His prophetic imagination was first displayed in pioneering works of science fiction such as *The Time Machine* (1895), *The Island of Doctor Moreau* (1896), *The Invisible Man* (1897) and *The War of the Worlds* (1898). Later he became an apostle of socialism, science and progress, whose anticipations of a future world state include *The Shape of Things to Come* (1933). His controversial views on sexual equality and women's rights were expressed in the novels *Ann Veronica* (1909) and *The New Machiavelli* (1911). He was, in Bertrand Russell's words, 'an important liberator of thought and action'.

Wells drew on his own early struggles in many of his best novels, including *Love and Mr Lewisham* (1900), *Kipps* (1905), *Tono-Bungay* (1909) and *The History of Mr Polly* (1910). His educational works, some written in collaboration, include *The Outline of History* (1920) and *The Science of Life* (1930). His *Experiment in Autobiography* (2 vols., 1934) reviews his world. He died in London in 1946.

PATRICK PARRINDER took his MA and Ph.D. at Cambridge University, where he held a Fellowship at King's College and published his first two books on Wells, *H. G. Wells* (1970) and *H. G. Wells: The Critical Heritage* (1972). He has been Chairman of the H. G. Wells Society and editor of *The Wellsian*, and has also written on James Joyce, science fiction, literary criticism and the history of the English novel. His book *Shadows of the Future* (1995) brings together his interests in Wells, science fiction and literary prophecy. Since 1986 he has been Professor of English at the University of Reading.

MARINA WARNER is a writer of fiction, history and criticism. Her studies of mythology and fairy tales include *Alone of All Her Sex: The Myth and the Cult of the Virgin Mary* (1976), *From the Beast to the Blonde* (1994) and *No Go the Bogeyman: Scaring, Lulling and Making Mock* (1998). In 1994 she gave the Reith Lectures on the BBC on the theme of 'Managing Monsters: Six Myths of Our Time'. Her most recent novel is *The Leto Bundle* (2001). She is a professor in the Department of Literature, Film and Theatre at the University of Essex, and is currently finishing a study of spirits and technologies, called *Figuring the Soul: From Waxworks to Ectoplasm*.

STEVEN MCLEAN has recently completed his Ph.D. in the Department of English Literature at the University of Sheffield. His thesis investigates the relationship between H. G. Wells's scientific romances and the discourses of science in the 1890s and early 1900s. Steven has published on Wells's early fiction. He is the current Secretary of the H. G. Wells Society.

H. G. WELLS

The Time Machine

Edited by PATRICK PARRINDER
With an Introduction by MARINA WARNER
and Notes by STEVEN MCLEAN

PENGUIN BOOKS

PENGUIN BOOKS

Published by the Penguin Group
Penguin Books Ltd, 80 Strand, London WC2R ORL, England
Penguin Group (USA) Inc., 375 Hudson Street, New York, New York 10014, USA
Penguin Group (Canada), 10 Alcorn Avenue, Toronto, Ontario, Canada M4V 3B2
(a division of Pearson Penguin Canada Inc.)
Penguin Ireland, 25 St Stephen's Green, Dublin 2, Ireland
(a division of Penguin Books Ltd)
Penguin Group (Australia), 250 Camberwell Road,
Camberwell, Victoria 3124, Australia (a division of Pearson Australia Group Pty Ltd)
Penguin Books India Pvt Ltd, 11 Community Centre,
Panchsheel Park, New Delhi – 110 017, India
Penguin Group (NZ), cnr Airborne and Rosedale Roads, Albany,
Auckland 1310, New Zealand (a division of Pearson New Zealand Ltd)
Penguin Books (South Africa) (Pty) Ltd, 24 Sturdee Avenue,
Rosebank 2196, South Africa

Penguin Books Ltd, Registered Offices: 80 Strand, London WC2R ORL, England

www.penguin.com

First published 1895
This edition first published in Penguin Classics 2005
13

Text copyright © the Literary Executors of the Estate of H. G. Wells
Biographical Note, Further Reading, Note on the Text copyright © Patrick Parrinder, 2005
Introduction copyright © Marina Warner, 2005
Notes copyright © Steven McLean, 2005
All rights reserved

The moral right of the editors has been asserted

Set in 10.25/12.25 pt PostScript Adobe Sabon
Typeset by Rowland Phototypesetting Ltd, Bury St Edmunds, Suffolk
Printed in England by Clays Ltd, St Ives plc

ISBN-13: 978–0–141–43997–6

www.greenpenguin.co.uk

Penguin Books is committed to a sustainable future
for our business, our readers and our planet.
The book in your hands is made from paper
certified by the Forest Stewardship Council.

CONTENTS

Biographical Note   vii
Introduction   xiii
Further Reading   xxix
Note on the Text   xxxi

THE TIME MACHINE   I

Appendix: Wells's Preface (1931)   93
Notes   97

Biographical Note

Herbert George Wells was born on 21 September 1866 at Bromley, Kent, a small market town soon to be swallowed up by the suburban growth of outer London. His father, formerly a professional gardener and a county cricketer renowned for his fast bowling, owned a small business in Bromley High Street selling china goods and cricket bats. The house was grandly known as Atlas House, but the centre of family life was a cramped basement kitchen underneath the shop. Soon Joseph Wells's cricketing days were cut short by a broken leg, and the family fortunes looked bleak.

Young 'Bertie' Wells had already shown great academic promise, but when he was thirteen, his family broke up and he was forced to earn his own living. His father was bankrupt, and his mother left home to become resident housekeeper at Uppark, the great Sussex country house where she had worked as a lady's maid before her marriage. Wells was taken out of school to follow his two elder brothers into the drapery trade. After serving briefly as a pupil-teacher and a pharmacist's assistant, in 1881 he was apprenticed to a department store in Southsea, working a thirteen-hour day and sleeping in a dormitory with his fellow-apprentices. This was the unhappiest period of his life, though he would later revisit it in comic romances such as *Kipps* (1905) and *The History of Mr Polly* (1910) Kipps and Polly both manage to escape from their servitude as drapers, and in 1883, helped by his long-suffering mother, Wells cancelled his indentures and obtained a post as teaching assistant at Midhurst Grammar School near Uppark. His intellectual development, long held back, now

progressed astonishingly. He passed a series of examinations in
science subjects and, in September 1884, entered the Normal
School of Science, South Kensington (later to become part of
Imperial College of Science and Technology) on a government
scholarship.

Wells was a born teacher, as many of his books would show,
and at first he was an enthusiastic student. He had the good
fortune to be taught biology and zoology by one of the most
influential scientific thinkers of the Victorian age, Darwin's
friend and supporter T. H. Huxley. Wells never forgot Huxley's
teaching, but the other professors were more humdrum, and
his interest in their courses rapidly waned. He scraped through
second-year physics, but failed his third-year geology exam and
left South Kensington in 1887 without taking a degree. He was
thrilled by the theoretical framework and imaginative horizons
of natural science, but impatient of practical detail and the
grinding, routine tasks of laboratory work. He cut his classes
and spent his time reading literature and history, satisfying the
curiosity he had earlier felt while exploring the long-neglected
library at Uppark. He started a college magazine, the *Science
Schools Journal*, and argued for socialism in student debates.

In the summer of 1887 Wells became science master at a
small private school in North Wales, but a few weeks later he
was knocked down and injured by one of his pupils on the
football field. Sickly and undernourished as a result of three
years of student poverty, he suffered severe kidney and lung
damage. After months of convalescence at Uppark he was able
to return to science teaching at Henley House School, Kilburn.
In 1890 he passed his University of London B.Sc. (Hons.) with
a first class in zoology and obtained a post as a biology tutor
for the University Correspondence College. In 1891 he married
his cousin Isabel Wells, but they had little in common and soon
Wells fell in love with one of his students, Amy Catherine
Robbins (usually known as 'Jane'). They started living together
in 1893, and married two years later when his divorce came
through.

During his years as a biology tutor Wells slowly began
making his way as a writer and journalist. He wrote for the

Educational Times, edited the *University Correspondent*, and in 1891 published a philosophical essay, 'The Rediscovery of the Unique', in the prestigious *Fortnightly Review*. His first book was a *Textbook of Biology* (1893). But no sooner was it published than his health again collapsed, forcing him to give up teaching and rely entirely on his literary earnings. His future seemed highly precarious, yet soon he was in regular demand as a writer of short stories and humorous essays for the burgeoning newspapers and magazines of the period. He became a fiction reviewer and, for a short period in 1895, a theatre critic.

Ever since his student days Wells had worked intermittently on a story about time-travelling and the possible future of the human race. An early version was published in the *Science Schools Journal* as 'The Chronic Argonauts', but now, after numerous redrafts and much encouragement from the poet and editor W. E. Henley, it finally took shape as *The Time Machine* (1895). Its success was instantaneous, and while it was running as a magazine serial Wells was already being spoken of as a 'man of genius'. He was celebrated as the inventor of the 'scientific romance', a combination of adventure novel and philosophical tale in which the hero becomes involved in a life-and-death struggle resulting from some unforeseen scientific development. There was now a ready market for his fiction, and *The Island of Doctor Moreau* (1896), *The Invisible Man* (1897), *The War of the Worlds* (1898), *When the Sleeper Wakes* (1899; later revised as *The Sleeper Awakes*, 1910), *The First Men in the Moon* (1901) and several other volumes followed quickly from his pen.

By the turn of the twentieth century Wells was established as a popular author in England and America, and his books were rapidly being translated into French, German, Spanish, Russian and other European languages. Already his fame had begun to eclipse that of his predecessor in scientific romance, the French author Jules Verne, who had dominated the field since the 1860s. But Wells, an increasingly self-conscious artist, had larger ambitions than to go down in history as a boys' adventure novelist like Jules Verne. *Love and Mr Lewisham* (1900) was his first attempt at realistic fiction, comic in spirit and manifestly reflecting his own experiences as a student and teacher. By the end of the Edwardian decade, when he wrote his 'Condition of England' novels *Tono-Bungay* (1909) and *The New Machiavelli* (1911), Wells had become one of the leading novelists of his day, the friend and rival of such literary figures as Arnold Bennett, Joseph Conrad, Ford Madox Ford and Henry James.

But Wells was never a devotee of art for art's sake; he was a prophetic writer with a social and political message. His first major non-fictional work was *Anticipations* (1902), a book of futurological essays setting out the possible effects of scientific and technological progress in the twentieth century. *Anticipations* brought him into contact with the Fabian Society and launched his career as a political journalist and an influential voice of the British left. During his Fabian period Wells wrote *A Modern Utopia* (1905), but failed in his attempt to challenge the bureaucratic, reformist outlook of the Society's leaders such as Bernard Shaw (a lifelong friend and rival) and Beatrice Webb. Wells's Edwardian scientific romances such as *The Food of the Gods* (1904) and *The War in the Air* (1908), though full of humorous touches, are propagandist in intent. In other 'future war' stories of this period he predicted the tank and the atomic bomb.

Success as an author brought about great changes in his personal life. Ill-health had forced him to leave London for the Kent coast in 1898, but in the long run the only legacy of his footballing injury was the diabetes that affected him in old age. He commissioned a house, Spade House, overlooking the English Channel at Sandgate, from the architect C. F. A. Voysey, and here his and Jane's two sons were born – George Philip or 'Gip', who became a zoology professor and collaborated with his father and Julian Huxley on the biology encyclopedia *The Science of Life* (1930), and Frank, who worked in the film industry. Wells gave generous support to his parents and to his eldest brother, who was a fellow-fugitive from the drapery trade. Increasingly, however, he looked for emotional fulfilment outside the family, and his sexual affairs became notorious. He had a daughter in 1909 with Amber Reeves, a leading young Fabian economist, and in 1914 the novelist and critic Rebecca

West gave birth to his son Anthony West, whose troubled childhood would later be reflected in his own novel *Heritage* (1955) and in his biography of his father.

As Wells's personal life became the gossip of literary London, his roles as imaginative writer and political journalist or prophet came increasingly into conflict. *Ann Veronica* (1909) was an example of topical, controversial fiction, dramatizing and commenting on such issues as women's rights, sexual equality and contemporary morals. It was the first of Wells's 'discussion novels' in which his personal relationships were often very thinly disguised. His later fiction takes a great variety of forms, but it all belongs to the broad category of the novel of ideas. At one extreme is the realistic reporting of *Mr Britling Sees It Through* (1916) – still valuable and unique as a portrayal of the English 'home front' in the First World War – while at the other extreme are brief fables such as *The Undying Fire* (1919) and *The Croquet Player* (1936), political allegories about world events each cast in the form of a prophetic dialogue.

Wells was by no means an experimental novelist like his younger contemporaries James Joyce and Virginia Woolf, but he was often technically innovative, and in some of his books the boundaries between fiction and non-fiction begin to break down. Sometimes he would take a classic from an earlier, pre-modern epoch as his literary model: *A Modern Utopia* (1905), for example, refers back to Sir Thomas More's *Utopia* and Plato's *Republic*. His bestselling historical works *The Outline of History* (1920) and *A Short History of the World* (1922) break with historical conventions by looking forward to the next stage in history. These works were written in order to draw the lessons of the First World War and to ensure that, if possible, its carnage would never be repeated; Wells saw history as a 'race between education and catastrophe'. The same concerns led to his future-history novel *The Shape of Things to Come* (1933), later rewritten for the cinema as *Things to Come*, an epic science-fiction film produced in 1936 by Alexander Korda. Both novel and film contain dire warnings about the inevitable outbreak and disastrous consequences of the Second World War.

By the 1920s, Wells was not only a famous author but a public figure whose name was rarely out of the newspapers. He briefly worked for the Ministry of Propaganda in 1918, producing a memorandum on war aims which anticipated the setting-up of the League of Nations. In 1922 and 1923 he stood for Parliament as a Labour candidate. He sought to influence world leaders, including two US presidents, Theodore Roosevelt and Franklin D. Roosevelt. His meeting with Lenin in the Kremlin in 1920 and his interview in 1934 with Lenin's successor Josef Stalin were publicized all over the world. His high-pitched, piping voice was often heard on BBC radio. In 1933 he was elected president of International PEN, the writers' organization campaigning for intellectual freedom. In the same year his books were publicly burnt by the Nazis in Berlin, and he was banned from visiting Fascist Italy. His ideas strongly influenced the Pan-European Union, the pressure group advocating European unity between the wars.

But Wells became convinced that nothing less than global unity was needed if humanity was not to destroy itself. In *The Open Conspiracy* (1928) and other books he outlined his theories of world citizenship and world government. As the Second World War drew nearer he felt that his mission had been a failure and his warnings had gone unheeded. His last great campaign, for which he tried to obtain international support, was for human rights. The proposal set out in his Penguin Special *The Rights of Man* (1940) helped to bring about the United Nations declaration of 1948. He spent the war years at his house in Hanover Terrace, Regent's Park, and was awarded a D.Sc. by London University in 1943. His last book, *Mind at the End of Its Tether* (1945), was a despairing, pessimistic work, even bleaker in its prospects for mankind than *The Time Machine* fifty years earlier. He died at Hanover Terrace on 13 August 1946. He was restless and tireless to the end, a prophet eternally dissatisfied with himself and with humanity. 'Some day', he had written in a whimsical 'Auto-Obituary' three years earlier, 'I shall write a book, a *real* book.' He had published over fifty works of fiction and, in total, some 150 books and pamphlets.

                                                    Patrick Parrinder

Introduction

Dreams and trance states used to be the principal, well-established methods of time travelling. Until Sigmund Freud published *The Interpretation of Dreams* in 1900, five years after H. G. Wells's *The Time Machine*, and defined them as fragments of desire and memories of the individual sleeper's unconscious, dreams had delivered warnings and portents for many different peoples and cultures; a gifted dreamer could communicate visions of the future and sometimes be understood: in the Bible Joseph in Egypt interprets Pharoah's prophetic dreams; in Roman history, as we hear from Shakespeare's *Julius Caesar*, Caesar's wife has a nightmare and tries to stop him going to the Senate on the day of his death. Precognition was supernatural rather than psychological, and certainly not scientific.

H. G. Wells is also a gifted dreamer, a 'wild talent',[1] a prophet, but in his great scientific romances of the late nineteenth century, he invented a new kind of storyteller and established a new kind of prophecy. No longer a sleeping or entranced visionary, a priestess in a cave or a saint on a rock, his seer was a man on the saddle of a kind of bicycle, customized in a suburban workshop, part crystal radio set, part clockwork, part points-switching railway tracks, part movie camera – the first Time Machine of modernity. With this device, Wells created far more than a fascinating narrative vehicle for his views of human destiny, cosmic history, class warfare, the evolution of sex and leisure and labour, and much else; his story has lasted as one of the most popular ever written, one of the most imitated and influential to this day, because it reaches out beyond the related episodes and ostensible plot to give us an image of human consciousness in potentia. The Time Machine in some deep sense does perform as Wells's own imagination, vaulting into aeons of futurity. It translates a faculty of mind – projective imagination – into an actual piece of technology, and embodies it physically in time and space. It is a Delphic tripod, a crystal ball, a stargazing lens, an I Ching trigram, but made to work in the age of the machine.

In the closing decades of the nineteenth century, the fascination with the involuntary workings of the mind was intense, and by no means confined to the most famous psychologist of the era, Sigmund Freud, and his theories of dreams and repression. For example, the Victorian novelist and thinker Samuel Butler formulated a theory of unconscious memory for a book with that title published in 1880, while, a little later, Frederic Myers, a strange but inspired writer on psychic and psychological matters, first came up with the theory of the 'subliminal self', which he saw as an influential repository of unconscious dreams and memories from previous lives and forgotten experiences. H. G. Wells dramatically transformed such speculations when he transposed mere mental voyaging into an actual vehicle; he gave an altogether new, exciting and persuasive meaning to the term 'out-of-the-body experience'. His machine offers an image of modern literature in action, of what writing can do through the words of an extraordinary and original fantasy at play. In yet another sense, *The Time Machine*'s archaeological plunge into the future replicates the incremental growth of language and meaning. When the philosophically minded French poet Paul Valéry came across Wells's story soon after it was published, he adapted Wells's device with great excitement to illuminate his ideas about the making of imagery itself through consciousness. He came to the conclusion that 'A symbol is something of a time machine. It's an inconceivable compression of the time taken by operations of the spirit . . .'[2] More than a decade before novelists started experimenting with the stream of consciousness, Wells grippingly dramatized his own powerful dream capacity to create symbols that leap across aeons of time, and made his visionary faculty itself appear to be the medium of an objective account of 'the shape of things to come'.

The Time Machine was the first of a dazzling sequence of inventions, which include *The Invisible Man*, *The Island of Doctor Moreau*, *The War of the Worlds* and 'The Plattner Story', published over a mere three years from 1895 to 1898. Wells has been called by Brian Aldiss the creator of a 'modern sublime'.[3] Generations of writers have continued the attempt to write in this vein: today, Wells is the progenitor of twenty-first-century cyber-sublime, even the godfather of cyberpunk. Together with Jorge Luis Borges, Wells could be said to be the first who gave us intimations of 'the force that's with us', who first found that 'the truth is out there', and imagined the concealed energy that powers the Matrix.

Astonishingly accurate in his predictions, Wells also achieved over the course of a long and extremely prolific career a rate of strike that few fortune-tellers, astrologers or dream diviners could match, in antiquity or now. His visions of aerial bombardment, chemical weapons, laser beams, industrial tourism, space travel, genetic engineering, cosmetic surgery, global warming and the vibrating universe, actually predate some of the most familiar features of our technological modern world: they precede even the radio and the first aeroplanes, for example, as well as the use of poison gas in the Great War. Meanwhile, the latest speculations of string theory and quantum mechanics have lit up new horizons for teleporters, mutation, cloning and other wonderful Wellsian speculations.[4]

Wells knew all about the vatic tradition, and he alludes now and then in his writing to oracles and prophets, to the sibylline utterances of antiquity and the visions of apocalypse in the Bible, and wrote to a friend when he was working on the final version of *The Time Machine*, 'it is the latest Delphic voice but the tripod is not broken.'[5] But his inspired move as a storyteller was to distance himself completely from the occult and the uncanny so prevalent in the fin de siècle when he started. Wells wrote – and published – several versions of the story which became *The Time Machine* from 1888 to 1895, and the powerful changes he introduced to his original idea of travelling into time reveal dramatically how he abandoned the supernatural and the uncanny as his fictional territory, and chose instead a new common manner of address that made him very much more provocative and exciting than his predecessors in utopian fabulism. 'The Chronic Argonauts' stays within the register of myth and antique fable, as its rather bombastic title shows, and it features a magician with a far-fetched name – Nebogipfel, cod German for 'mist-wrapped mountain' – closer to the tradition of mystification and esoterica.[6] Wells was no stranger to this literature: he invoked as one of his influences Lucian of Samosata, the great master of comic and prurient magic, as well as his follower and imitator Apuleius, and his *Metamorphosis, or The Golden Ass*, a wondrous concatenation of transmogrifications, spells and grotesque misadventures. Rather nearer to Wells's own time, the speed and directness used by Edgar Allan Poe in his tales of the supernatural clearly shaped Wells's own storytelling manner; but while these masters continued to colour the fantastic of M. R. James and H. P. Lovecraft, Wells parted from them very significantly. He is not looking to give his readers the thrill of the paranormal or to make us shiver at the mysteries of the unknown; he rather presents marvels as knowable, introduces us to wonders of nature and the universe as revealed by reason. Poe makes us tremble at the clock ticking under the floor; Robert Louis Stevenson learned the art of the 'good crawler' from the tales of Scottish faerie and weirdness that his nurse told him when he was a child ill in bed; Lovecraft also makes our flesh crawl at the rats scratching in the wall; and Henry James, stepping into this haunted territory, most effectively conjures the shivers and the pleasures of unexplained phenomena and irrational malignancy in *The Turn of the Screw*. By contrast, when H. G. Wells throws open vistas (a word he likes), he wants to persuade us that the world on the other side of the door that he opens is not a personal delusion but a scientific truth that can be explained.

In Wells's 'scientific romances', a popular genre ('Tales of the Unexpected') meets and combines with others in a unique fusion: he was writing not only during the same period as many masters of the shudder and the thrill, but in the aftermath of an extraordinarily fecund period for children's fantastic literature, utopian fictions and traveller's yarns. The expansion of the British empire spread through the closing decades of the century accompanied by a polyphony of storytelling, like a Greek chorus commenting on the action, now in pride, now in horror. Wells listened in on these voices to great effect: in *The Time Machine* the pluck and aggressiveness of the protagonist as he battles for survival against the dread and loathsome Morlocks with little more than a nearly spent box of safety matches as weapon, match up to action heroes in imperial adventures of deadly perils, as in G. A. Henty and Rider Haggard (*King Solomon's Mines*, 1886, and *She*, 1887).

When the Traveller first lands in the future, beside the looming winged statue of the White Sphinx, that decaying monument of a vanished civilization, the effect brings to mind an exotic location far from Richmond; the Palace of Green Porcelain, which the Traveller discovers later, also evokes distant, subjugated territories which sent a pagoda to Kew Gardens, as well as an obelisk and an assortment of sphinxes to the Embankment in London.[7] But Victorian wealth and power instigated another kind of literature, a fugue of the imagination into a myriad invented Nowheres, Elsewheres, Wonderlands and Outlands. The impulse to reconfigure social realities in dream geographies moved reforming Christian idealists like Charles Kingsley, with his underwater haven (*The Water Babies*, 1863), George Mac-Donald, who conjured his chivalrous, fairy realms (*At the Back of the North Wind*, 1871), as well as Tennyson and his poetic voyaging through the Arthurian cycle *The Idylls of the King*. Even Lewis Carroll with Wonderland and Looking-Glass country develops, through Alice's eyes and nonsense inversions, alternatives to the adult society of arbitrary laws, tyrannical rulers and double talk. Peter Pan's Never-Never Land is a Utopia out of the Victorian nursery tradition, where many of the conditions that created Victorian power have been specifically overturned, and no one has to be good or diligent or work or suffer hardship or cruelty or poverty or indignity or subordination to an owner or a boss.

The children's writers have retained huge audiences and international readership, whereas some of the adult visionaries are perhaps now studied more than enjoyed. Wells was himself inspired directly by two important contributions to the tradition: Samuel Butler's *Erewhon* (1872) and William Morris's *News From Nowhere* (1890). Both these fantasies of possible other worlds were the products of highly gifted and unusual men with a very wide range of interests and activities and a restless drive towards reform and utopia: Butler was a pioneering photographer and psychologist as well as a satirical novelist, and in his book he savaged the progress of the world as he saw it. His Erewhon (nowhere spelled backwards) is a topsy-turvy world, where being ill is a crime and all disease concealed for fear of punishment, while unreason is worshipped without question. Butler was responding, and Wells would follow his example, to the dangers implicit in Darwin's view of human survival in *The Origin of Species*. By contrast, William Morris was a much softer optimist and dreamer, a founder of the Pre-Raphaelites, an embattled Socialist, a master printer, poet and painter, and the famous and successful champion of the arts and crafts movement; through his wallpapers and fabrics, he created the aesthetic most closely identified with the look and quality of Victorian design. Morris also wrote in the shadow cast by Darwin and Butler, but the dream society of *News from Nowhere or An Epoch of Rest being some chapters from a Utopian Romance* pictures humanity happily regressed into an idyllic, de-industrialized pastorale where modernity has been superseded. His paragons live in a medieval time warp of manual crafts. Both Butler's and Morris's Nowheres are glimpsed in *The Time Machine*, for Wells explicitly takes up issues these predecessors raise, and dramatizes their contrasting viewpoints through the Morris-like Eloi and the Butler-like Morlocks. He also adopted the brilliant switch of perspective Morris had used when he projected the traditional 'once upon a time' into the future.

The freshness of Wells's storytelling arises from this new realist tone, which has not a little touch of the deliberately banal. (In his story 'The Argonauts of the Air', a dazzling prophecy of air travel, he writes of the building of the aeroplane: 'Through the grove of iron pillars . . . one had a glimpse of the pretty scenery towards Esher' – a most typical and assured effect of queering the ordinary.)[8] As in *The Time Machine*, his favoured locale is the leafy suburbs around London, his favoured milieu ordinary people of the middle to lower middle class, and his discourse by choice matter-of-fact, objective and scientific. He winds up our excitement by placing wild events in this familiar landscape: it is a strategy that inverts the usual far-fetched material of fantasy into seemingly 'near-fetched' observation. For Wells there is only physics to give the texture of the reality in his stories, the canny is far preferable to the uncanny, yet the effect on the reader immerses us in a deeper and more vertiginously disorientating metaphysics.

The Time Machine is a long short story, or novella, in twelve parts with an epilogue; it folds its stories about the future within a frame story in the style of oral narrative; an 'Outside Narrator', clearly not an interested party and more sober and reliable than the inventor, can persuade us more fully of what happened. The chronology of the enchained stories is elaborate, contributing to the general pent-up excitement which the successive eyewitness narratives arouse. The plot falls into three sections: it opens in the inventor's house, in medias res at a dinner party, during which he explains his theory of the fourth dimension, time, and shows his guests a little model of his invention, a 'beautifully made' machine which can voyage through time as if through space. One of the guests trips the lever, and thus sends this model out on its journey in time: it vanishes from the table (and does not return). Someone introduces the possibility of conjuring but this is dashed down instantly. 'I am absolutely certain there was no trickery,' the narrator tells us.

A week later, at a second gathering of guests, the Time Traveller appears, dishevelled, haggard, with bleeding feet, and tells them of his voyage to the year 802,701 and of his experiences – at first wonderful, then terrible – with the descendants of humanity in the future. This part contains the richest and

most eventful dramatic action in the story, including the land-
ing near the White Sphinx, the encounters with the Eloi, his
loving attachment to Weena, and the near-fatal battle with the
Morlocks. The emotion veers wildly, from bouts of pulp-fiction
aggression to Sunday-school pastoral sentiment. In the third
part, the Time Traveller describes how he then precipitated
himself faster and deeper into time and, in an apocalyptic vision
recalling medieval allegories of divine retribution, beheld the
end of the universe in a general darkness, with only one monstrous round thing, hopping, with tentacles trailing 'against the
red water of the sea'. Finally, in a laconic and melancholy
Epilogue, the narrator tells us that the Traveller set out again
three years before and has still not returned.

The last decade of Queen Victoria's reign, when Wells was
making up his pioneering scientific romances, was an era of
unsurpassed scientific discovery, and many Victorian scientists
were developing the technologies that would create the modern world. Electromagnetism, radio waves, X-rays, new gases
(neon, argon, crypton, xenon) brought modernity into being
(submarine cables were connecting the world, cities were illuminated, moving pictures started, followed by the telephone and,
later, by television). All these innovations created a climate of
excited possibility: if images and sounds could be moved over
great distances, might it not be imaginable to move thoughts
and objects as well? In 1882, two years before H. G. Wells
began studying at the Normal School of Science in South
Kensington, a group of leading philosophers and scientists
founded the Society for Psychical Research in order to investigate all kinds of unexplained phenomena. Surprising as it may
seem, their attitude was determinedly scientific and positivist as
they embarked in a spirit of solemn and sceptical rationality on
experiments in telepathy, teleportation, telekinesis and other
possibilities.

The framing scene of *The Time Machine* in the Inventor's
Richmond house captures the kind of social setting in which
the SPR conducted its activities, and even reproduces some of
the effects of their seances, when the Psychologist sends the first
time machine, the inventor's small prototype, on its way into

the future: 'There was a breath of wind, and the lamp flame jumped. One of the candles on the mantel was blown out, and the little machine suddenly swung round, became indistinct, was seen as a ghost for a second perhaps . . . and it was gone – vanished!'

Later, when the Time Traveller returns from the future, he finds two large white flowers crushed in his pocket; these are of an unknown species and they prove to him and to his listeners that he had experienced no dream but had truly lived with the Eloi in their garden of Eden. Similarly, the researchers of the Society set great store by the 'apports', often gifts of flowers, which mediums materialized during seances and gave to sitters (Elizabeth Barrett Browning, at a gathering at a friend's house in Ealing with the famous medium Daniel Dunglas Home, was delighted when he placed a garland on her head, supposedly conjured from the other side). The name of the housekeeper in *The Time Machine*, Mrs Watchett, even hints with a touch of Wellsian comedy at a scene of nocturnal carryings-on, or mediumship.

Victorian speculations into psychic science continued to interest Wells, for he concludes his magisterial and hugely successful encyclopedic study of biology, *The Science of Life* (1930) with detailed accounts of 'borderlands', hypnotism and multiple personality, and even reproduces photographs of mediums emitting ectoplasm. However, the crucial point to make about this association is that the SPR's heavily scientific methods of investigation offered a different way of thinking and writing about weird and wonderful phenomena. In 1933, reflecting with disarming frankness on his most famous and successful fictions, H. G. Wells explained his technique: 'For the writer of fantastic stories to help the reader play the game properly, he must help him in every possible unobtrusive way to *domesticate* the impossible hypothesis. He must trick him into an unwary concession to get some plausible assumption and get on with the story while the illusion holds. And that is why there was a slight novelty in my stories when they first appeared. Hitherto, except in exploration fantasies, the fantastic element was brought in by magic . . . It occurred to me that

... an ingenious use of scientific patter might with advantage be substituted.'[9]

Wells was working as a science journalist while writing *The Time Machine*, and began exploring the idea in a series of articles, not stories, during its first appearances in magazines. The story condenses preoccupations that began in Wells's childhood, when he first encountered cosmology, biology and ethics of human behaviour in the library of Uppark where his mother worked 'below stairs'; there he saw illustrations of Extinct Animals, which made a lasting impression, and read – among other things – Bunyan's *Pilgrim's Progress* and Swift's *Gulliver's Travels*. He managed to gain a bursary to study in South Kensington under the celebrated Darwinian Thomas H. Huxley and attended his lectures on evolution; Huxley remained a profound influence and imaginary interlocutor throughout his writing life, for Wells continued to struggle, in both his fiction and his historical writings, with the implications of natural selection for human society. Huxley argued, for example, 'Social progress means a checking of the cosmic process at every step and the substitution for it of another, which may be called the ethical process; the end of which is not the survival of those who may happen to be the fittest ... but of those who are ethically the best.'[10] In the same spirit, Wells's buoyancy grew when he imagined something could be done to halt entropy (human degeneration, dog-eats-dog, cosmic cooling), but he was engulfed in darkness and despair (as in *The Time Machine*) when he envisaged the inevitable effects of natural selection developing unchecked.

The Time Machine's vision of the future issues a stark warning of the outcome for the human race: the Traveller first meets the dainty, fragile, pretty, childish Upperworld people, who idle their days away in flowering meadows, live on fruit, spend their days dancing and playfully making love, have forgotten how to read and write, and no longer even understand the properties of fire. These are the Eloi, and their name echoes with 'elite', and also with 'elohim' (Lord and God in Hebrew). He rescues one of the Eloi women from drowning, and as his friendship with the infantile Weena becomes closer he discovers the reason for the terror the Eloi suffer. The human species has evolved into two distinct subspecies: below ground, in a deep lightless system of tunnels and shafts and mines, live the Morlocks, partly blind and greyish-white from lack of exposure to the light, but still intelligent, tool-using creatures who toil and produce. The Morlocks' name catches echoes of 'warlock', but it too resonates with biblical terms, including Moloch, the obscene god of the Canaanites, who exacts child sacrifices on his altars (II Kings 23:10). It gradually becomes clear to the Traveller that the Morlocks prey on the Eloi: the Eloi's flowering garden is a pasture, where, like pretty little baa-lambs, they frolic and graze before being taken down to the Morlocks' subterranean tunnels. The Time Traveller's love has the belittling name Weena, enclosing 'wean', which impresses on the reader her helpless nursling character. But a 'weaner' is also a young animal, a calf or piglet or lamb, and somehow the associations between the Morlocks' abominable eating habits and Weena's death in a fire inadvertently suggest a fate Wells is too squeamish to make plain. Indeed the Traveller tells himself (deludes himself?) that Weena has simply been lost in the forest fire that he himself started.

This compelling and gruesome vision of human destiny grew in H. G. Wells's imagination in connection with two powerful tendencies in Victorian science: first, the Victorians' passion for machines of all kinds, which led them to export inventions – from cameras to cables to aeroplanes – all over the world, and secondly, the continuing post-Darwinian argument about survival, about individualism versus collectivism, and the consequent conflict between post-Romantic views of the single person, and Socialist or Universalist ideals of community and ecology.

The first tendency brought the Time Machine into existence: it is the latest creation of the Time Traveller, who, we learn in the story's very first paragraph, has designed the dining-room chairs which 'embraced and caressed us rather than submitted to be sat upon'. This visionary ergonomic furniture sets the scene for the much more ambitious prosthesis, the Time Machine itself. Samuel Butler towards the end of *Erewhon* includes a chapter called 'The Book of Machines'. There, Butler pushes mechanical materialism to extremes, and elaborates an implacable vision of nature, society, and humans' place within them, describing eyes as 'little see-engines'[11] and declaring that 'Man's very soul is due to the machines; it is a machine-made thing . . .'[12]

Wells was deeply struck by Butler's nightmarish and satirical dystopia: the Time Traveller's plan to take Weena with him back to his past echoes the flight of Butler's protagonist with his Erewhon love, Arowhena; but whereas Butler's lovers succeed in escaping in a spectacular balloon ascent, Wells's Time Traveller loses Weena, as we saw. One of the several touches of ghastliness that makes *The Time Machine* peculiarly startling occurs when the Traveller returns and demands, before he tells his guests anything about his travels, 'Save me some of that mutton. I'm starving for a bit of meat.' The food chain obsessed Wells; as a post-Darwinian biologist he himself gnaws at the problem of human survival.[13] In the nightmare future Wells imagines, the Morlocks have reverted to cannibalism ('the old habit') and the Eloi have become 'their fatted cattle'. But after Weena's death, the Traveller's lust for mutton on re-entry to his own time does strike a jarring note and aligns him with the Morlocks, those predators upon the innocent and paschal Eloi.

The concept of 'Man' as a 'machinate mammal' took strong hold of Wells, and he can be seen struggling to steel himself to the concept of human inhumanity throughout his work from *The Time Machine*'s distress onwards. He shows an almost anorexic fascination with feeding, hunger and abstemiousness; in several stories he devised all kinds of outlandish varieties of food supply in order to circumvent it. In the article 'Man in the Year Million', written before *The Time Machine*, he fantasticated a future when human beings would have become brains swimming in vats, nourished by some chemical elixir, and in *The War of the Worlds* the hero's tactics to obtain food interplay with brilliantly intricate accounts of the Martians' means of sustenance. Once more, they are described as cannibal predators, heads without bodies, interfused with their fantastic fighting-machines, which, like giant mosquitoes, they inject with their quarry's blood as if oiling an engine. Wells was not alone in brooding on alternative, utopian strategies to emancipate humans from the generic stain of hunting, killing and carnivorousness. In Edward Bulwer-Lytton's curious prophetic novel *The Coming Race* (1871), the super-evolved people of the future have achieved their status through a potion called vril, a kind of mesmeric fluid-cum-death-ray-cum-serum-cum-nectar-cum-Viagra. (In 1889, the manufacturers of a product intended to endow its consumers with equally magic powers of health, stamina, strength, virility and so forth, added 'vril' to 'bos' (Latin for ox) and came up with Bovril!)[14]

The equivalence he drew between animate and inanimate forms did not stop at food consumption. *The Science of Life* opens with a chapter resoundingly entitled 'The Body is a Machine', and declares, 'A petrol motor, or a fire, does exactly the same [as a human body]; in both cases, besides fuel, there must be a supply of air ... The living organism so far as its energy-output is concerned is really and precisely a combustion engine ... Indeed, the whole of what we have called the fundamental round of Mr Everyman is a mechanical process.'[15] There is an insistence to this kind of drawn-out metaphor that reveals Wells trying to convince himself, much as the Time Traveller argues with himself that it is only natural the Morlocks should have taken the path they have. In the stories, much of the superb tension of the narrative voice grows from Wells's oscillation between his radical scientific view and his apocalyptic despair. He seems to be struggling with himself through his protagonists towards a vision that will provide an alternative to the doom in plain sight, but his honesty forces him back to admit that there are no grounds for hope. Like nursery tales of ogres and ballads about serial murderers, some of Wells's future visions belong in the category of tale that invents the worst case in order to prevent it, and Huxley's insistence on the necessity of ethics spurred his imaginative manoeuvres.

Meat provides one focal metaphor for this pessimism, about 'nature red in tooth and claw', or Evolution in action; by contrast, china offers an opposite point of identification, an image of possible effects of society, culture and even ethics. But these are, like china, fragile and offer only feeble dreams, in much the same way as a willow-pattern plate presents a fanciful vision of far Cathay: the Eloi enjoy a 'Dresden-china type of prettiness', and the Traveller and Weena drift into the Palace of Green Porcelain, the ruins of a Kensington museum, with 'decaying vestiges of books' silently announcing the futility of learning and literature. The Traveller finds some matches: he rescues fire from the ruins of our civilization, a future Prometheus.

The drama of the bestial Morlocks, toiling underground, blind, larval and yet overpoweringly strong, vividly and repellently conjure the oppressed from a Victorian reformer's tract – Engels on the working masses, Dickens's protests – while, as many have pointed out, the enfeebled and pleasure-loving Eloi embody a spoiled aristocracy: the Dresden-china image bringing to mind Marie Antoinette playing the shepherdess. In an early, revolutionary version of the story, the subterranean labourers rise against their Upperworld oppressors; in yet another the latter rule by hypnosis – both rather Marxist plotlines. But in the end, Wells abandoned this kind of agitprop for science, his true interest, and took a very long view. Extinction, not renewal, was to be the ultimate outcome.

His dark vision has captivated readers far more than any uplifting tale of class struggle could have achieved. Yet Wells loves illumination and floods his stories with sunlight, often imagining paradises within reach of some fabulous instrument, though tantalizingly elusive. In another of his famous tales, the sensitive and dreamlike story 'The Door in the Wall', his hero Wallace once found, when he was a child, a bright, summer refuge through a green door: 'there was something in the sight of it that made all its colour clean and perfect and subtly luminous . . . everything was beautiful there . . .'. But Wallace has not been able to find this vision again. Wells's radical, progressive scientific optimism, glimpsing a future where everything might be beautiful, clashed with a despairing fatalism and sense of loss, both in his own nature and his literary vision. The dazzle of light in his writings often becomes a blaze devastating the universe, just as the sunlit meadows of the future are consumed in flames in *The Time Machine*, and later, in the sublime apocalypse thirty million years hence, 'the huge red-hot dome of sun' dies and the Time Traveller sees the world blacked out into bitter, cold darkness. The vigour and pace of the story and its tough, resolute Time Traveller carry all the different themes and arguments of the story with unsurpassed storytelling skill, but Wells conveys how close he felt to the melancholy seeker after a door that he once opened on to a luminous vision and could never find again.

Marina Warner

NOTES

1. Charles Fort, Victorian scholar and collector of esoterica, called mediums, especially children with psycho-kinetic powers, 'wild talents'.

2. Paul Valéry, *Mauvaises Pensées et autres* III, *Mercure de France* 30 (May 1899), in Paul Valéry, *Oeuvres* (Paris, 1983), p. 1461.

3. Brian W. Aldiss, 'Doomed Formicary versus the Technological Sublime', in *H. G. Wells's Perennial Time Machine*, ed. George Slusser, Patrick Parrinder, Danièle Chatelain (Athens, Georgia, and London, 2001), p. 189.

4. See Brian Greene, *The Fabric of the Cosmos: Space, Time and the Texture of Reality* (London, 2004).

5. Letter to Elizabeth Healey, in Geoffrey West, *H. G. Wells: A Sketch for a Portrait* (London, 1930), p. 77; see also Patrick Parrinder, *Shadows of the Future: H. G. Wells, Science Fiction and Prophecy* (Liverpool, 1995), pp. 18–33.

6. For example, the magician and tutor of Alexander the Great in *The Romance of Alexander* (third century BCE) is called Nectanebo; H. G. Wells, 'The Chronic Argonauts', in *The Definitive Time Machine*, ed. Harry M. Geduld (Bloomington, IN, 1987), pp. 135–52.

7. The pagoda at Kew Gardens opened to the public in the 1870s, and Cleopatra's Needle was installed in 1878, with accompanying Egyptian motifs, including splendid sphinx benches, along the Embankment.

8. *The Short Stories of H. G. Wells* (London, [1927]; 1952), pp. 346–58.

9.   H. G. Wells, *Seven Famous Novels* (New York, 1934), p. viii.

10. T. H. Huxley, 'Evolution and Ethics', Romanes Lecture (1893), quoted in James Gunn, *The Science of Science Fiction Writing* (Lanham, Maryland, 2000), www.ku.edu/~sfcenter/tomorrow.htm

11. Samuel Butler, *Erewhon*, ed. Peter Mudford (London, 1970; 1985) p. 205.

12. Butler, *Erewhon*, p. 207.

13. See Peter Kemp, *H. G. Wells and the Culminating Ape: Biological Themes and Imaginative Obsessions* (London [1982]; 1996) pp. 12–15.

14. John Carey (ed.), *The Faber Book of Utopias* (London, 1999), p. 261.

15. H. G. Wells, Julian Huxley, G. P. Wells, *The Science of Life* (London, 1931), 2 vols. Vol. 1, p. 22.

Further Reading

The most vivid and memorable account of Wells's life and times is his own *Experiment in Autobiography* (2 vols., London: Gollancz and Cresset Press, 1934). It has been reprinted several times. A 'postscript' containing the previously suppressed narrative of his sexual liaisons was published as *H. G. Wells in Love*, edited by his son G. P. Wells (London: Faber & Faber, 1984). His more recent biographers draw on this material, as well as on the large body of letters and personal papers archived at the University of Illinois and elsewhere. The fullest and most scholarly biographies are *The Time Traveller* by Norman and Jeanne Mackenzie (2nd edn, London: Hogarth Press, 1987) and *H. G. Wells: Desperately Mortal* by David C. Smith (New Haven and London: Yale University Press, 1986). Smith has also edited a generous selection of Wells's *Correspondence* (4 vols., London: Pickering & Chatto, 1998). Another highly readable, if controversial and idiosyncratic, biography is *H. G. Wells: Aspects of a Life* (London: Hutchinson, 1984) by Wells's son Anthony West. Michael Foot's *H. G.: The History of Mr Wells* (London and New York: Doubleday, 1995) is enlivened by its author's personal knowledge of Wells and his circle.

Two illuminating general interpretations of Wells and his writings are Michael Draper's *H. G. Wells* (Basingstoke: Macmillan, 1987) and Brian Murray's *H. G. Wells* (New York: Continuum, 1990). Both are introductory in scope, but Draper's approach is critical and philosophical, while Murray packs a remarkable amount of biographical and historical detail into a short space. John Hammond's *An H. G. Wells Companion* (London and Basingstoke: Macmillan, 1979) and

H. G. Wells (Harlow and London: Longman, 2001) combine criticism with useful contextual material. *H. G. Wells: The Critical Heritage*, edited by Patrick Parrinder (London: Routledge, 1972), is a collection of reviews and essays of Wells published during his lifetime. A number of specialized critical and scholarly studies of Wells concentrate on his scientific romances. These include Bernard Bergonzi's pioneering study of *The Early H. G. Wells* (Manchester: Manchester University Press, 1961); John Huntington, *The Logic of Fantasy: H. G. Wells and Science Fiction* (New York: Columbia University Press, 1982); and Patrick Parrinder, *Shadows of the Future: H. G. Wells, Science Fiction and Prophecy* (Liverpool: Liverpool University Press, 1995). Peter Kemp's *H. G. Wells and the Culminating Ape* (London and Basingstoke: Macmillan, 1982) offers a lively and, at times, lurid tracing of Wells's 'biological themes and imaginative obsessions', while Roslynn D. Haynes's *H. G. Wells: Discoverer of the Future* (London and Basingstoke: Macmillan, 1980) surveys his use of scientific ideas. W. Warren Wagar, *H. G. Wells and the World State* (New Haven: Yale University Press, 1961) and John S. Partington, *Building Cosmopolis* (Aldershot: Ashgate, 2003) are studies of his political thought and his schemes for world government. John S. Partington has also edited *The Wellsian* (The Netherlands: Equilibris, 2003), a selection of essays from the H. G. Wells Society's annual critical journal of the same name. The American branch of the Wells Society maintains a highly informative website at http://hgwellsusa.50megs.com

P. P.

Note on the Text

H. G. Wells's first story based on the idea of a time machine was 'The Chronic Argonauts', begun while he was a student at South Kensington and published in three instalments in the *Science Schools Journal* (April–June 1888). After several rewritings, an unfinished version of *The Time Machine* appeared in seven instalments in the *National Observer* under the editorship of the poet W. E. Henley, beginning in March 1894. The serialization was abruptly discontinued in June by Henley's editorial successor, but a few months later the poet became editor of the *New Review* and encouraged Wells to produce a revised and expanded version of *The Time Machine*. This appeared as a monthly serial in the *New Review* between January and May 1895, attracting considerable publicity even before its publication in book form by William Heinemann in London in May. The Heinemann edition is subtitled 'An Invention' and dedicated to Henley. A slightly earlier version, credited to 'H. S. Wells' on the title-page, was published in the same month by Henry Holt in New York. Holt excludes the Epilogue, but includes a brief 'kangaroo and centipede' episode in what would become section 11 of the present text. This episode was deleted from all subsequent texts.

Although the original Heinemann text remained in print throughout its author's lifetime and beyond, Wells noted down a number of small changes in 1898 or 1899. These were eventually incorporated into what he called his 'revised definitive version' of *The Time Machine* in Volume I of the Atlantic Edition of the Works of H. G. Wells (London: T. Fisher Unwin, and New York: Scribner's, 1924). A few further corrections were added, however, to later reprints. Thus in 1927 the Atlantic text of *The Time Machine* appeared in Wells's *Complete Short Stories* and also in volume 16 of the collected Essex edition of Wells's works, both published by Ernest Benn. Of the two versions, that in the *Complete Short Stories* is closer to the 1931 de luxe Random House edition of *The Time Machine* (with illustrations by W. A. Dwiggins), which brings together Wells's post-Atlantic revisions. The new preface that Wells wrote in 1931 is reprinted as an Appendix in the present volume.

Since the post-Atlantic reprints of *The Time Machine* were not, in general, proof-read to the same high standard as the Atlantic text, the present edition follows the latter, corrected against the Random House edition and with the modifications set out below. Later reprints during Wells's lifetime, including the 1935 Everyman edition which is the basis of the 1995 Everyman edition edited by John Lawton, do not improve on the Random House text. The first Penguin edition of *The Time Machine* was prepared during Wells's lifetime, though not published until a few weeks after his death in 1946. This was a reprint of the 1895 Heinemann text. Subsequently, however, a version of the Atlantic text, with corrections based on Benn's *Complete Short Stories*, appeared in the Penguin volume of Wells's *Selected Short Stories*, first published in 1958 and much reprinted. This was, arguably, closer to Wells's final intentions than any of its predecessors except Random House.

The principal difference between the Atlantic and Heinemann texts is Wells's reduction of Heinemann's 16 chapters to 12 sections and his deletion of the chapter titles. The fact that Wells chose to include *The Time Machine* in his *Complete Short Stories* suggests that he had come to regard it as an expanded tale or novella, rather than a novel divided into named chapters. In the present text, each of sections 1, 4, 5 and 12 incorporates two of Heinemann's original chapters. The original chapter titles, which are sometimes cited in criticism of *The Time Machine*, were as follows: I Introduction; II The Machine; III The Time Traveller Returns; IV Time Travelling; V In the Golden Age; VI The Sunset of Mankind; VII A Sudden Shock;

VIII Explanation; IX The Morlocks; X When the Night Came; XI The Palace of Green Porcelain; XII In the Darkness; XIII The Trap of the White Sphinx; XIV The Further Vision; XV The Time Traveller Returns; XVI After the Story. (Chapter XVI includes the Epilogue.)

The substantive emendations to the Atlantic text in the present edition are listed with their sources below. The following abbreviations have been used: H = Heinemann, Ho = Holt, MS = manuscript, R = Random House.

Page:line	Reading adopted	Atlantic reading rejected
22:26	wings (R)	wins
28:32	situated (R)	situate
32:17	is (H, R)	in
37:4	behoves (R)	behooves
50:1	of the human (R)	of human [H has 'of her human']
54:2	Upperworld	Over-world [R has 'Upper-world']
73:15	spat (MS)	split [Ho has 'spit']
78:13	Upperworld	Over-world [R has 'Upper-world']

The Random House revisions of 'Over-world' to 'Upper-world' make consistent a change that Wells had introduced elsewhere in the Atlantic text; otherwise, the Atlantic readings listed are identical to all earlier texts except where indicated. The manuscript reading of 'spat' for 'split' or 'spit' was brought to light by Professor David Lake.

Further changes in the present text are the substitution of 'leapt' for 'leaped', 'anyone' for 'any one', 'someone' for 'some one', 'everyday' for 'every day', 'someday' for 'some day', etc. Hyphens have been removed from such words as 'all-fours', 'blood-stained', 'egg-shell', 'head-lines', 'nine-pins', 'to-night', 'to-morrow', and 'Upper-world', in accordance with modern practice.

Housestyling of punctuation and spelling has also been implemented to make the text more accessible to the reader:

single quotation marks (for doubles) with doubles inside singles as needed; end punctuation placed outside end quotation marks when appropriate; spaced N-dashes (for the heavier, longer M-dash) and M-dashes (for the double-length 2M-dash); 'iz' spellings (e.g. recognize, not recognise), and acknowledgements and judgement, not acknowledgments and judgment; no full stop after personal titles (Dr, Mr, Mrs).

The textual prehistory of *The Time Machine* is well represented in *The Definitive Time Machine: A Critical Edition of H. G. Wells's Scientific Romance*, ed. Harry M. Geduld (Bloomington and Indianapolis: Indiana University Press, 1987). Geduld reprints both 'The Chronic Argonauts' and the *National Observer* serialization in full, but treats the 1924 Atlantic edition as if it contained Wells's final revisions. The manuscripts of *The Time Machine* in the Wells Collection at the Rare Book and Special Collections Library, University of Illinois at Urbana-Champaign, show Wells's development of the story from the *National Observer* version to its publication in book form. A number of pages of manuscript and corrected typescript are reproduced in facsimile in Bernard Loing, *H. G. Wells à l'oeuvre: les débuts d'un écrivain (1894–1900)* (Paris: Didier, 1984). Other scholars to whose work on the texts of *The Time Machine* I am greatly indebted include David Lake and Bernard Bergonzi.

P. P.

THE TIME MACHINE

The Time Traveller (for so it will be convenient to speak of him) was expounding a recondite matter to us. His grey eyes shone and twinkled, and his usually pale face was flushed and animated. The fire burned brightly, and the soft radiance of the incandescent lights in the lilies of silver caught the bubbles that flashed and passed in our glasses. Our chairs, being his patents, embraced and caressed us rather than submitted to be sat upon, and there was that luxurious after-dinner atmosphere when thought runs gracefully free of the trammels of precision. And he put it to us in this way – marking the points with a lean forefinger – as we sat and lazily admired his earnestness over this new paradox (as we thought it) and his fecundity.

'You must follow me carefully. I shall have to controvert one or two ideas that are almost universally accepted. The geometry, for instance, they taught you at school is founded on a misconception.'

'Is not that rather a large thing to expect us to begin upon?' said Filby, an argumentative person with red hair.

'I do not mean to ask you to accept anything without reasonable ground for it. You will soon admit as much as I need from you. You know of course that a mathematical line, a line of thickness *nil*, has no real existence. They taught you that? Neither has a mathematical plane. These things are mere abstractions.'

'That is all right,' said the Psychologist.

'Nor, having only length, breadth and thickness, can a cube have a real existence.'

'There I object,' said Filby. 'Of course a solid body may exist. All real things —'

'So most people think. But wait a moment. Can an *instantaneous* cube exist?'

'Don't follow you,' said Filby.

'Can a cube that does not last for any time at all, have a real existence?'

Filby became pensive. 'Clearly,' the Time Traveller proceeded, 'any real body must have extension in *four* directions: it must have Length, Breadth, Thickness and – Duration. But through a natural infirmity of the flesh, which I will explain to you in a moment, we incline to overlook this fact. There are really four dimensions, three which we call the three planes of Space, and a fourth, Time. There is, however, a tendency to draw an unreal distinction between the former three dimensions and the latter, because it happens that our consciousness moves intermittently in one direction along the latter from the beginning to the end of our lives.'

'That,' said a very young man, making spasmodic efforts to relight his cigar over the lamp; 'that . . . very clear indeed.'

'Now, it is very remarkable that this is so extensively overlooked,' continued the Time Traveller, with a slight accession of cheerfulness. 'Really this is what is meant by the Fourth Dimension, though some people who talk about the Fourth Dimension do not know they mean it. It is only another way of looking at Time. *There is no difference between Time and any of the three dimensions of Space except that our consciousness moves along it*. But some foolish people have got hold of the wrong side of that idea. You have all heard what they have to say about this Fourth Dimension?'

'*I* have not,' said the Provincial Mayor.

'It is simply this. That Space, as our mathematicians have it, is spoken of as having three dimensions, which one may call Length, Breadth and Thickness, and is always definable by reference to three planes, each at right angles to the others. But some philosophical people have been asking why *three* dimensions particularly – why not another direction at right angles to the other three? – and have even tried to construct a Four-Dimensional geometry. Professor Simon Newcomb was expounding this to the New York Mathematical Society only a month or so ago.[1] You know how on a flat surface, which has only two dimensions, we can represent a figure of a three-dimensional solid, and similarly they think that by models of three dimensions they could represent one of four – if they could master the perspective of the thing. See?'

'I think so,' murmured the Provincial Mayor; and, knitting his brows, he lapsed into an introspective state, his lips moving as one who repeats mystic words. 'Yes, I think I see it now,' he said after some time, brightening in a quite transitory manner.

'Well, I do not mind telling you I have been at work upon this geometry of Four Dimensions for some time. Some of my results are curious. For instance, here is a portrait of a man at eight years old, another at fifteen, another at seventeen, another at twenty-three and so on. All these are evidently sections, as it were, Three-Dimensional representations of his Four-Dimensioned being, which is a fixed and unalterable thing.

'Scientific people,' proceeded the Time Traveller, after the pause required for the proper assimilation of this, 'know very well that Time is only a kind of Space. Here is a popular scientific diagram, a weather record. This line I trace with my finger shows the movement of the barometer. Yesterday it was so high, yesterday night it fell, then this morning it rose again, and so gently upward to here. Surely the mercury did not trace this line in any of the dimensions of Space generally recognized? But certainly it traced such a line, and that line, therefore, we must conclude was along the Time-Dimension.'

'But,' said the Medical Man, staring hard at a coal in the fire, 'if Time is really only a fourth dimension of Space, why is it, and why has it always been, regarded as something different? And why cannot we move about in Time as we move about in the other dimensions of Space?'

The Time Traveller smiled. 'Are you so sure we can move freely in Space? Right and left we can go, backward and forward freely enough, and men always have done so. I admit we move freely in two dimensions. But how about up and down? Gravitation limits us there.'

'Not exactly,' said the Medical Man. 'There are balloons.'

'But before the balloons, save for spasmodic jumping and the inequalities of the surface, man had no freedom of vertical movement.'

'Still they could move a little up and down,' said the Medical Man.

'Easier, far easier down than up.'

'And you cannot move at all in Time, you cannot get away from the present moment.'

'My dear sir, that is just where you are wrong. That is just where the whole world has gone wrong. We are always getting away from the present moment. Our mental existences, which are immaterial and have no dimensions, are passing along the Time-Dimension with a uniform velocity from the cradle to the grave. Just as we should travel *down* if we began our existence fifty miles above the earth's surface.'

'But the great difficulty is this,' interrupted the Psychologist. 'You *can* move about in all directions of Space, but you cannot move about in Time.'

'That is the germ of my great discovery. But you are wrong to say that we cannot move about in Time. For instance, if I am recalling an incident very vividly I go back to the instant of its occurrence: I become absent-minded, as you say. I jump back for a moment. Of course we have no means of staying back for any length of time, any more than a savage or an animal has of staying six feet above the ground. But a civilized man is better off than the savage in this respect. He can go up against gravitation in a balloon, and why should he not hope that ultimately he may be able to stop or accelerate his drift along the Time-Dimension, or even turn about and travel the other way?'

'Oh, *this*,' began Filby, 'is all —'

'Why not?' said the Time Traveller.

'It's against reason,' said Filby.

'What reason?' said the Time Traveller.

'You can show black is white by argument,' said Filby, 'but you will never convince me.'

'Possibly not,' said the Time Traveller. 'But now you begin to see the object of my investigations into the geometry of Four

Dimensions. Long ago I had a vague inkling of a machine—'

'To travel through Time!' exclaimed the Very Young Man.

'That shall travel indifferently in any direction of Space and Time, as the driver determines.'

Filby contented himself with laughter.

'But I have experimental verification,' said the Time Traveller.

'It would be remarkably convenient for the historian,' the Psychologist suggested. 'One might travel back and verify the accepted account of the Battle of Hastings,[2] for instance!'

'Don't you think you would attract attention?' said the Medical Man. 'Our ancestors had no great tolerance for anachronisms.'

'One might get one's Greek from the very lips of Homer and Plato,' the Very Young Man thought.

'In which case they would certainly plough you for the Little-go.[3] The German scholars have improved Greek so much.'

'Then there is the future,' said the Very Young Man. 'Just think! One might invest all one's money, leave it to accumulate at interest, and hurry on ahead!'

'To discover a society,' said I, 'erected on a strictly communistic basis.'

'Of all the wild extravagant theories!' began the Psychologist.

'Yes, so it seemed to me, and so I never talked of it until—'

'Experimental verification!' cried I. 'You are going to verify *that*?'

'The experiment!' cried Filby, who was getting brain-weary.

'Let's see your experiment anyhow,' said the Psychologist, 'though it's all humbug, you know.'

The Time Traveller smiled round at us. Then, still smiling faintly, and with his hands deep in his trousers pockets, he walked slowly out of the room, and we heard his slippers shuffling down the long passage to his laboratory.

The Psychologist looked at us. 'I wonder what he's got?'

'Some sleight-of-hand trick or other,' said the Medical Man, and Filby tried to tell us about a conjurer he had seen at Burslem;[4] but before he had finished his preface the Time Traveller came back, and Filby's anecdote collapsed.

The thing the Time Traveller held in his hand was a glittering metallic framework, scarcely larger than a small clock, and very delicately made. There was ivory in it, and some transparent crystalline substance. And now I must be explicit, for this that follows – unless his explanation is to be accepted – is an absolutely unaccountable thing. He took one of the small octagonal tables that were scattered about the room, and set it in front of the fire, with two legs on the hearth rug. On this table he placed the mechanism. Then he drew up a chair, and sat down. The only other object on the table was a small shaded lamp, the bright light of which fell full upon the model. There were also perhaps a dozen candles about, two in brass candlesticks upon the mantel and several in sconces, so that the room was brilliantly illuminated. I sat in a low armchair nearest the fire, and I drew this forward so as to be almost between the Time Traveller and the fireplace. Filby sat behind him, looking over his shoulder. The Medical Man and the Provincial Mayor watched him in profile from the right, the Psychologist from the left. The Very Young Man stood behind the Psychologist. We were all on the alert. It appears incredible to me that any kind of trick, however subtly conceived and however adroitly done, could have been played upon us under these conditions.

The Time Traveller looked at us, and then at the mechanism. 'Well?' said the Psychologist.

'This little affair,' said the Time Traveller, resting his elbows upon the table and pressing his hands together above the apparatus, 'is only a model. It is my plan for a machine to travel through time. You will notice that it looks singularly askew, and that there is an odd twinkling appearance about this bar, as though it was in some way unreal.' He pointed to the part with his finger. 'Also, here is one little white lever, and here is another.'

The Medical Man got up out of his chair and peered into the thing. 'It's beautifully made,' he said.

'It took two years to make,' retorted the Time Traveller. Then, when we had all imitated the action of the Medical Man, he said: 'Now I want you clearly to understand that this lever, being pressed over, sends the machine gliding into the future, and this other reverses the motion. This saddle represents the seat of a time traveller. Presently I am going to press the lever, and off the machine will go. It will vanish, pass into future Time and disappear. Have a good look at the thing. Look at the table too, and satisfy yourselves there is no trickery. I don't want to waste this model, and then be told I'm a quack.'

There was a minute's pause perhaps. The Psychologist seemed about to speak to me, but changed his mind. Then the Time Traveller put forth his finger towards the lever. 'No,' he said suddenly. 'Lend me your hand.' And turning to the Psychologist, he took that individual's hand in his own and told him to put out his forefinger. So that it was the Psychologist himself who sent forth the model Time Machine on its interminable voyage. We all saw the lever turn. I am absolutely certain there was no trickery. There was a breath of wind, and the lamp flame jumped. One of the candles on the mantel was blown out, and the little machine suddenly swung round, became indistinct, was seen as a ghost for a second perhaps, as an eddy of faintly glittering brass and ivory; and it was gone – vanished! Save for the lamp the table was bare.

Everyone was silent for a minute. Then Filby said he was damned.

The Psychologist recovered from his stupor, and suddenly looked under the table. At that the Time Traveller laughed cheerfully. 'Well?' he said, with a reminiscence of the Psychologist. Then, getting up, he went to the tobacco jar on the mantel, and with his back to us began to fill his pipe.

We stared at each other. 'Look here,' said the Medical Man, 'are you in earnest about this? Do you seriously believe that that machine has travelled into time?'

'Certainly,' said the Time Traveller, stooping to light a spill at the fire. Then he turned, lighting his pipe, to look at the Psychologist's face. (The Psychologist, to show that he was not unhinged, helped himself to a cigar and tried to light it uncut.) 'What is more, I have a big machine nearly finished in there' – he indicated the laboratory – 'and when that is put together I mean to have a journey on my own account.'

'You mean to say that that machine has travelled into the future?' said Filby.

'Into the future or the past – I don't, for certain, know which.'

After an interval the Psychologist had an inspiration. 'It must have gone into the past if it has gone anywhere,' he said.

'Why?' said the Time Traveller.

'Because I presume that it has not moved in space, and if it travelled into the future it would still be here all this time, since it must have travelled through this time.'

'But,' said I, 'if it travelled into the past it would have been visible when we came first into this room; and last Thursday when we were here; and the Thursday before that; and so forth!'

'Serious objections,' remarked the Provincial Mayor, with an air of impartiality, turning towards the Time Traveller.

'Not a bit,' said the Time Traveller, and, to the Psychologist: 'You think. *You* can explain that. It's presentation below the threshold, you know, diluted presentation.'

'Of course,' said the Psychologist, and reassured us. 'That's a simple point of psychology. I should have thought of it. It's plain enough, and helps the paradox delightfully. We cannot see it, nor can we appreciate this machine, any more than we can the spoke of a wheel spinning, or a bullet flying through the air. If it is travelling through time fifty times or a hundred times faster than we are, if it gets through a minute while we get through a second, the impression it creates will of course be only one-fiftieth or one-hundredth of what it would make if it were not travelling in time. That's plain enough.' He passed his hand through the space in which the machine had been. 'You see?' he said, laughing.

We sat and stared at the vacant table for a minute or so. Then the Time Traveller asked us what we thought of it all.

'It sounds plausible enough tonight,' said the Medical Man; 'but wait until tomorrow. Wait for the common sense of the morning.'

'Would you like to see the Time Machine itself?' asked the Time Traveller. And therewith, taking the lamp in his hand, he led the way down the long, draughty corridor to his laboratory.

I remember vividly the flickering light, his queer, broad head in silhouette, the dance of the shadows, how we all followed him, puzzled but incredulous, and how there in the laboratory we beheld a larger edition of the little mechanism which we had seen vanish from before our eyes. Parts were of nickel, parts of ivory, parts had certainly been filed or sawn out of rock crystal. The thing was generally complete, but the twisted crystalline bars lay unfinished upon the bench beside some sheets of drawings, and I took one up for a better look at it. Quartz it seemed to be.

'Look here,' said the Medical Man, 'are you perfectly serious? Or is this a trick – like that ghost you showed us last Christmas?'

'Upon that machine,' said the Time Traveller, holding the lamp aloft, 'I intend to explore time. Is that plain? I was never more serious in my life.'

None of us quite knew how to take it.

I caught Filby's eye over the shoulder of the Medical Man, and he winked at me solemnly.

2

I think that at that time none of us quite believed in the Time Machine. The fact is, the Time Traveller was one of those men who are too clever to be believed: you never felt that you saw all round him; you always suspected some subtle reserve, some ingenuity in ambush, behind his lucid frankness. Had Filby shown the model and explained the matter in the Time Traveller's words, we should have shown *him* far less scepticism. For we should have perceived his motives: a pork butcher could understand Filby. But the Time Traveller had more than a touch of whim among his elements, and we distrusted him. Things that would have made the fame of a less clever man seemed tricks in his hands. It is a mistake to do things too easily. The serious people who took him seriously never felt quite sure of his deportment: they were somehow aware that trusting their reputations for judgement with him was like furnishing a nursery with eggshell china. So I don't think any of us said very much about time travelling in the interval between that Thursday and the next, though its odd potentialities ran, no doubt, in most of our minds: its plausibility, that is, its practical incredibleness, the curious possibilities of anachronism and of utter confusion it suggested. For my own part, I was particularly preoccupied with the trick of the model. That I remember discussing with the Medical Man, whom I met on Friday at the Linnaean.[1] He said he had seen a similar thing at Tübingen,[2] and laid considerable stress on the blowing out of the candle. But how the trick was done he could not explain.

The next Thursday I went again to Richmond [3] – I suppose I was one of the Time Traveller's most constant guests – and, arriving late, found four or five men already assembled in his drawing-room. The Medical Man was standing before the fire with a sheet of paper in one hand and his watch in the other. I looked round for the Time Traveller, and – 'It's half past seven now,' said the Medical Man. 'I suppose we'd better have dinner?'

'Where's—?' said I, naming our host.

'You've just come? It's rather odd. He's unavoidably detained. He asks me in this note to lead off with dinner at seven if he's not back. Says he'll explain when he comes.'

'It seems a pity to let the dinner spoil,' said the Editor of a well-known daily paper; and thereupon the Doctor rang the bell.

The Psychologist was the only person besides the Doctor and myself who had attended the previous dinner. The other men were Blank, the Editor aforementioned, a certain journalist and another – a quiet, shy man with a beard – whom I didn't know, and who, as far as my observation went, never opened his mouth all the evening. There was some speculation at the dinner table about the Time Traveller's absence, and I suggested time travelling, in a half jocular spirit. The Editor wanted that explained to him, and the Psychologist volunteered a wooden account of the 'ingenious paradox and trick' we had witnessed that day week. He was in the midst of his exposition when the door from the corridor opened slowly and without noise. I was facing the door, and saw it first. 'Hallo!' I said. 'At last!' And the door opened wider, and the Time Traveller stood before us. I gave a cry of surprise. 'Good heavens! man, what's the matter?' cried the Medical Man, who saw him next. And the whole tableful turned towards the door.

He was in an amazing plight. His coat was dusty and dirty, and smeared with green down the sleeves; his hair disordered, and as it seemed to me greyer – either with dust and dirt or because its colour had actually faded. His face was ghastly pale; his chin had a brown cut on it – a cut half healed; his expression was haggard and drawn, as by intense suffering. For a moment he hesitated in the doorway, as if he had been dazzled by the light. Then he came into the room. He walked with just such a limp as I have seen in footsore tramps. We stared at him in silence, expecting him to speak.

He said not a word, but came painfully to the table, and made a motion towards the wine. The Editor filled a glass of champagne, and pushed it towards him. He drained it, and it seemed to do him good: for he looked round the table, and the ghost of his old smile flickered across his face. 'What on earth have you been up to, man?' said the Doctor. The Time Traveller did not seem to hear. 'Don't let me disturb you,' he said, with a certain faltering articulation. 'I'm all right.' He stopped, held out his glass for more, and took it off at a draught. 'That's good,' he said. His eyes grew brighter, and a faint colour came into his cheeks. His glance flickered over our faces with a certain dull approval, and then went round the warm and comfortable room. Then he spoke again, still as it were feeling his way among his words. 'I'm going to wash and dress, and then I'll come down and explain things. . . . Save me some of that mutton. I'm starving for a bit of meat.'

He looked across at the Editor, who was a rare visitor, and hoped he was all right. The Editor began a question. 'Tell you presently,' said the Time Traveller. 'I'm – funny! Be all right in a minute.'

He put down his glass, and walked towards the staircase door. Again I remarked his lameness and the soft padding sound of his footfall, and standing up in my place, I saw his feet as he went out. He had nothing on them but a pair of tattered, bloodstained socks. Then the door closed upon him. I had half a mind to follow, till I remembered how he detested any fuss about himself. For a minute, perhaps, my mind was wool gathering. Then, 'Remarkable Behaviour of an Eminent Scientist,' I heard the Editor say, thinking (after his wont) in headlines. And this brought my attention back to the bright dinner table.

'What's the game?' said the Journalist. 'Has he been doing the Amateur Cadger?[4] I don't follow.' I met the eye of the Psychologist, and read my own interpretation in his face. I thought of the Time Traveller limping painfully upstairs. I don't think anyone else had noticed his lameness.

The first to recover completely from this surprise was the

Medical Man, who rang the bell – the Time Traveller hated to have servants waiting at dinner – for a hot plate. At that the Editor turned to his knife and fork with a grunt, and the Silent Man followed suit. The dinner was resumed. Conversation was exclamatory for a little while, with gaps of wonderment; and then the Editor got fervent in his curiosity. 'Does our friend eke out his modest income with a crossing? or has he his Nebuchadnezzar phases?'[5] he inquired. 'I feel assured it's this business of the Time Machine,' I said, and took up the Psychologist's account of our previous meeting. The new guests were frankly incredulous. The Editor raised objections. 'What *was* this time travelling? A man couldn't cover himself with dust by rolling in a paradox, could he?' And then, as the idea came home to him, he resorted to caricature. Hadn't they any clothes-brushes in the Future? The Journalist, too, would not believe at any price, and joined the Editor in the easy work of heaping ridicule on the whole thing. They were both the new kind of journalist – very joyous, irreverent young men.[6] 'Our Special Correspondent in the Day after Tomorrow reports,' the Journalist was saying – or rather shouting – when the Time Traveller came back. He was dressed in ordinary evening clothes, and nothing save his haggard look remained of the change that had startled me.

'I say,' said the Editor hilariously, 'these chaps here say you have been travelling into the middle of next week!! Tell us all about little Rosebery,[7] will you? What will you take for the lot?'

The Time Traveller came to the place reserved for him without a word. He smiled quietly, in his old way. 'Where's my mutton?' he said. 'What a treat it is to stick a fork into meat again!'

'Story!' cried the Editor.

'Story be damned!' said the Time Traveller. 'I want something to eat. I won't say a word until I get some peptone[8] into my arteries. Thanks. And the salt.'

'One word,' said I. 'Have you been time travelling?'

'Yes,' said the Time Traveller, with his mouth full, nodding his head.

'I'd give a shilling a line for a verbatim note,'[9] said the Editor. The Time Traveller pushed his glass towards the Silent Man and rang it with his fingernail; at which the Silent Man, who had been staring at his face, started convulsively, and poured him wine. The rest of the dinner was uncomfortable. For my own part, sudden questions kept on rising to my lips, and I dare say it was the same with the others. The Journalist tried to relieve the tension by telling anecdotes of Hettie Potter.[10] The Time Traveller devoted his attention to his dinner, and displayed the appetite of a tramp. The Medical Man smoked a cigarette, and watched the Time Traveller through his eyelashes. The Silent Man seemed even more clumsy than usual, and drank champagne with regularity and determination out of sheer nervousness. At last the Time Traveller pushed his plate away, and looked round us. 'I suppose I must apologize,' he said. 'I was simply starving. I've had a most amazing time.' He reached out his hand for a cigar, and cut the end. 'But come into the smoking-room. It's too long a story to tell over greasy plates.' And ringing the bell in passing, he led the way into the adjoining room.

'You have told Blank, and Dash, and Chose about the machine?' he said to me, leaning back in his easy chair and naming the three new guests.

'But the thing's a mere paradox,' said the Editor.

'I can't argue tonight. I don't mind telling you the story, but I can't argue. I will,' he went on, 'tell you the story of what has happened to me, if you like, but you must refrain from interruptions. I want to tell it. Badly. Most of it will sound like lying. So be it! It's true – every word of it, all the same. I was in my laboratory at four o'clock, and since then . . . I've lived eight days . . . such days as no human being ever lived before! I'm nearly worn out, but I shan't sleep till I've told this thing over to you. Then I shall go to bed. But no interruptions! Is it agreed?'

'Agreed,' said the Editor, and the rest of us echoed 'Agreed.' And with that the Time Traveller began his story as I have set it forth. He sat back in his chair at first, and spoke like a weary man. Afterwards he got more animated. In writing it down I feel with only too much keenness the inadequacy of pen and ink – and, above all, my own inadequacy – to express its quality. You read, I will suppose, attentively enough; but you cannot see the speaker's white, sincere face in the bright circle of the little lamp, nor hear the intonation of his voice. You cannot know how his expression followed the turns of his story! Most of us hearers were in shadow, for the candles in the smoking-room had not been lighted, and only the face of the Journalist and the legs of the Silent Man from the knees downward were illuminated. At first we glanced now and again at each other. After a time we ceased to do that, and looked only at the Time Traveller's face.

3

'I told some of you last Thursday of the principles of the Time Machine, and showed you the actual thing itself, incomplete in the workshop. There it is now, a little travel-worn, truly; and one of the ivory bars is cracked, and a brass rail bent; but the rest of it's sound enough. I expected to finish it on Friday; but on Friday, when the putting together was nearly done, I found that one of the nickel bars was exactly one inch too short, and this I had to get remade; so that the thing was not complete until this morning. It was at ten o'clock today that the first of all Time Machines began its career. I gave it a last tap, tried all the screws again, put one more drop of oil on the quartz rod, and sat myself in the saddle. I suppose a suicide who holds a pistol to his skull feels much the same wonder at what will come next as I felt then. I took the starting lever in one hand and the stopping one in the other, pressed the first, and almost immediately the second. I seemed to reel; I felt a nightmare sensation of falling; and, looking round, I saw the laboratory exactly as before. Had anything happened? For a moment I suspected that my intellect had tricked me. Then I noted the clock. A moment before, as it seemed, it had stood at a minute or so past ten; now it was nearly half past three!

'I drew a breath, set my teeth, gripped the starting lever with both hands, and went off with a thud. The laboratory got hazy and went dark. Mrs Watchett came in and walked, apparently without seeing me, towards the garden door. I suppose it took her a minute or so to traverse the place, but to me she seemed to shoot across the room like a rocket. I pressed the lever over to its extreme position. The night came like the turning out of a lamp, and in another moment came tomorrow. The laboratory grew faint and hazy, then fainter and ever fainter. Tomorrow night came black, then day again, night again, day again, faster and faster still. An eddying murmur filled my ears, and a strange, dumb confusedness descended on my mind.

'I am afraid I cannot convey the peculiar sensations of time travelling. They are excessively unpleasant. There is a feeling exactly like that one has upon a switchback – of a helpless headlong motion! I felt the same horrible anticipation, too, of an imminent smash. As I put on pace, night followed day like the flapping of a black wing. The dim suggestion of the laboratory seemed presently to fall away from me, and I saw the sun hopping swiftly across the sky, leaping it every minute, and every minute marking a day. I supposed the laboratory had been destroyed and I had come into the open air. I had a dim impression of scaffolding, but I was already going too fast to be conscious of any moving things. The slowest snail that ever crawled dashed by too fast for me. The twinkling succession of darkness and light was excessively painful to the eye. Then, in the intermittent darknesses, I saw the moon spinning swiftly through her quarters from new to full, and had a faint glimpse of the circling stars. Presently, as I went on, still gaining velocity, the palpitation of night and day merged into one continuous greyness; the sky took on a wonderful deepness of blue, a splendid luminous colour like that of early twilight; the jerking sun became a streak of fire, a brilliant arch, in space; the moon a fainter fluctuating band; and I could see nothing of the stars, save now and then a brighter circle flickering in the blue.

'The landscape was misty and vague. I was still on the hillside upon which this house now stands, and the shoulder rose above me grey and dim. I saw trees growing and changing like puffs of vapour, now brown, now green; they grew, spread, shivered, and passed away. I saw huge buildings rise up faint and fair, and pass like dreams. The whole surface of the earth seemed changed – melting and flowing under my eyes. The little hands upon the dials that registered my speed raced round faster and faster. Presently I noted that the sun belt swayed up and down, from solstice to solstice, in a minute or less, and that consequently my pace was over a year a minute; and minute by minute the white snow flashed across the world, and vanished, and was followed by the bright, brief green of spring.

'The unpleasant sensations of the start were less poignant now. They merged at last into a kind of hysterical exhilaration. I remarked indeed a clumsy swaying of the machine, for which I was unable to account. But my mind was too confused to attend to it, so with a kind of madness growing upon me, I flung myself into futurity. At first I scarce thought of stopping, scarce thought of anything but these new sensations. But presently a fresh series of impressions grew up in my mind – a certain curiosity and therewith a certain dread – until at last they took complete possession of me. What strange developments of humanity, what wonderful advances upon our rudimentary civilization, I thought, might not appear when I came to look nearly into the dim elusive world that raced and fluctuated before my eyes! I saw great and splendid architecture rising about me, more massive than any buildings of our own time, and yet, as it seemed, built of glimmer and mist. I saw a richer green flow up the hillside, and remain there without any wintry intermission. Even through the veil of my confusion the earth seemed very fair. And so my mind came round to the business of stopping.

'The peculiar risk lay in the possibility of my finding some substance in the space which I, or the machine, occupied. So long as I travelled at a high velocity through time, this scarcely mattered; I was, so to speak, attenuated – was slipping like a vapour through the interstices of intervening substances! But to come to a stop involved the jamming of myself, molecule by molecule, into whatever lay in my way; meant bringing my atoms into such intimate contact with those of the obstacle that a profound chemical reaction – possibly a far-reaching explosion – would result, and blow myself and my apparatus out of all possible dimensions – into the Unknown. This possibility had occurred to me again and again while I was making the machine; but then I had cheerfully accepted it as an unavoidable risk – one of the risks a man has got to take! Now the risk was inevitable, I no longer saw it in the same cheerful light. The fact is that, insensibly, the absolute strangeness of everything, the sickly jarring and swaying of the machine, above all, the feeling of prolonged falling, had absolutely upset my nerve. I told myself that I could never stop, and with a gust of petulance I resolved to stop forthwith. Like an impatient fool, I lugged over the lever, and incontinently the thing went reeling over, and I was flung headlong through the air.

'There was the sound of a clap of thunder in my ears. I may have been stunned for a moment. A pitiless hail was hissing round me, and I was sitting on soft turf in front of the overset machine. Everything still seemed grey, but presently I remarked that the confusion in my ears was gone. I looked round me. I was on what seemed to be a little lawn in a garden, surrounded by rhododendron bushes, and I noticed that their mauve and purple blossoms were dropping in a shower under the beating of the hailstones. The rebounding, dancing hail hung in a cloud over the machine, and drove along the ground like smoke. In a moment I was wet to the skin. "Fine hospitality," said I, "to a man who has travelled innumerable years to see you."

'Presently I thought what a fool I was to get wet. I stood up and looked round me. A colossal figure, carved apparently in some white stone, loomed indistinctly beyond the rhododendrons through the hazy downpour. But all else of the world was invisible.

'My sensations would be hard to describe. As the columns of hail grew thinner, I saw the white figure more distinctly. It was very large, for a silver birch-tree touched its shoulder. It was of white marble, in shape something like a winged sphinx,[1] but the wings, instead of being carried vertically at the sides, were spread so that it seemed to hover. The pedestal, it appeared to me, was of bronze, and was thick with verdigris. It chanced that the face was towards me; the sightless eyes seemed to watch me; there was the faint shadow of a smile on the lips. It was greatly weather-worn, and that imparted an unpleasant suggestion of disease. I stood looking at it for a little space – half a minute, perhaps, or half an hour. It seemed to advance and to recede as the hail drove before it denser or thinner. At last I tore my eyes from it for a moment, and saw that the hail curtain had worn threadbare, and that the sky was lightening with the promise of the sun.

'I looked up again at the crouching white shape, and the full temerity of my voyage came suddenly upon me. What might appear when that hazy curtain was altogether withdrawn? What might not have happened to men? What if cruelty had grown into a common passion? What if in this interval the race had lost its manliness, and had developed into something inhuman, unsympathetic, and overwhelmingly powerful? I might seem some old-world savage animal, only the more dreadful and disgusting for our common likeness – a foul creature to be incontinently slain.

'Already I saw other vast shapes – huge buildings with intricate parapets and tall columns, with a wooded hillside dimly creeping in upon me through the lessening storm. I was seized with a panic fear. I turned frantically to the Time Machine, and strove hard to readjust it. As I did so the shafts of the sun smote through the thunderstorm. The grey downpour was swept aside and vanished like the trailing garments of a ghost. Above me, in the intense blue of the summer sky, some faint brown shreds of cloud whirled into nothingness. The great buildings about me stood out clear and distinct, shining with the wet of the thunderstorm, and picked out in white by the unmelted hailstones piled along their courses. I felt naked in a strange world. I felt as perhaps a bird may feel in the clear air, knowing the hawk wings above and will swoop. My fear grew to frenzy. I took a breathing space, set my teeth, and again grappled fiercely, wrist and knee, with the machine. It gave under my desperate onset and turned over. It struck my chin violently. One hand on the saddle, the other on the lever, I stood panting heavily in attitude to mount again.

'But with this recovery of a prompt retreat my courage recovered. I looked more curiously and less fearfully at this world of the remote future. In a circular opening, high up in the wall of the nearer house, I saw a group of figures clad in rich soft robes. They had seen me, and their faces were directed towards me.

'Then I heard voices approaching me. Coming through the bushes by the White Sphinx were the heads and shoulders of men running. One of these emerged in a pathway leading straight to the little lawn upon which I stood with my machine. He was a slight creature – perhaps four feet high – clad in a purple tunic, girdled at the waist with a leather belt. Sandals or buskins – I could not clearly distinguish which – were on his feet; his legs were bare to the knees, and his head was bare. Noticing that, I noticed for the first time how warm the air was.

'He struck me as being a very beautiful and graceful creature, but indescribably frail. His flushed face reminded me of the more beautiful kind of consumptive – that hectic beauty of which we used to hear so much. At the sight of him I suddenly regained confidence. I took my hands from the machine.

4

'In another moment we were standing face to face, I and this fragile thing out of futurity. He came straight up to me and laughed into my eyes. The absence from his bearing of any sign of fear struck me at once. Then he turned to the two others who were following him and spoke to them in a strange and very sweet and liquid tongue.

'There were others coming, and presently a little group of perhaps eight or ten of these exquisite creatures were about me. One of them addressed me. It came into my head, oddly enough, that my voice was too harsh and deep for them. So I shook my head, and, pointing to my ears, shook it again. He came a step forward, hesitated, and then touched my hand. Then I felt other soft little tentacles upon my back and shoulders. They wanted to make sure I was real. There was nothing in this at all alarming. Indeed, there was something in these pretty little people that inspired confidence – a graceful gentleness, a certain childlike ease. And besides, they looked so frail that I could fancy myself flinging the whole dozen of them about like ninepins. But I made a sudden motion to warn them when I saw their little pink hands feeling at the Time Machine. Happily then, when it was not too late, I thought of a danger I had hitherto forgotten, and reaching over the bars of the machine I unscrewed the little levers that would set it in motion, and put these in my pocket. Then I turned again to see what I could do in the way of communication.

'And then, looking more nearly into their features, I saw some further peculiarities in their Dresden-china type of prettiness. Their hair, which was uniformly curly, came to a sharp end at the neck and cheek; there was not the faintest suggestion of it on the face, and their ears were singularly minute. The mouths were small, with bright red, rather thin lips, and the little chins ran to a point. The eyes were large and mild; and – this may seem egotism on my part – I fancied even then that there was a certain lack of the interest I might have expected in them.

'As they made no effort to communicate with me, but simply stood round me smiling and speaking in soft cooing notes to each other, I began the conversation. I pointed to the Time Machine and to myself. Then, hesitating for a moment how to express time, I pointed to the sun. At once a quaintly pretty little figure in chequered purple and white followed my gesture, and then astonished me by imitating the sound of thunder.

'For a moment I was staggered, though the import of his gesture was plain enough. The question had come into my mind abruptly: were these creatures fools? You may hardly understand how it took me. You see I had always anticipated that the people of the year Eight Hundred and Two Thousand odd would be incredibly in front of us in knowledge, art, everything. Then one of them suddenly asked me a question that showed him to be on the intellectual level of one of our five-year-old children – asked me, in fact, if I had come from the sun in a thunderstorm! It let loose the judgement I had suspended upon their clothes, their frail light limbs and fragile features. A flow of disappointment rushed across my mind. For a moment I felt that I had built the Time Machine in vain.

'I nodded, pointed to the sun, and gave them such a vivid rendering of a thunderclap as startled them. They all withdrew a pace or so and bowed. Then came one laughing towards me, carrying a chain of beautiful flowers altogether new to me, and put it about my neck. The idea was received with melodious applause; and presently they were all running to and fro for flowers, and laughingly flinging them upon me until I was almost smothered with blossom. You who have never seen the like can scarcely imagine what delicate and wonderful flowers countless years of culture had created. Then someone suggested that their plaything should be exhibited in the nearest building, and so I was led past the sphinx of white marble, which had seemed to watch me all the while with a smile at my astonishment, towards a vast grey edifice of fretted stone. As I went with them the memory of my confident anticipations of a profoundly grave and intellectual posterity came, with irresistible merriment, to my mind.

'The building had a huge entry, and was altogether of colossal dimensions. I was naturally most occupied with the growing crowd of little people, and with the big open portals that yawned before me shadowy and mysterious. My general impression of the world I saw over their heads was of a tangled waste of beautiful bushes and flowers, a long-neglected and yet weedless garden. I saw a number of tall spikes of strange white flowers, measuring a foot perhaps across the spread of the waxen petals. They grew scattered, as if wild, among the variegated shrubs, but, as I say, I did not examine them closely at this time. The Time Machine was left deserted on the turf among the rhododendrons.

'The arch of the doorway was richly carved, but naturally I did not observe the carving very narrowly, though I fancied I saw suggestions of old Phoenician decorations[1] as I passed through, and it struck me that they were very badly broken and weather-worn. Several more brightly clad people met me in the doorway, and so we entered, I, dressed in dingy nineteenth-century garments, looking grotesque enough, garlanded with flowers, and surrounded by an eddying mass of bright, soft-coloured robes and shining white limbs, in a melodious whirl of laughter and laughing speech.

'The big doorway opened into a proportionately great hall hung with brown. The roof was in shadow, and the windows, partially glazed with coloured glass and partially unglazed, admitted a tempered light. The floor was made up of huge blocks of some very hard white metal, not plates nor slabs, blocks, and it was so much worn, as I judged by the going to and fro of past generations, as to be deeply channelled along the more frequented ways. Transverse to the length were innumerable tables made of slabs of polished stone, raised perhaps a foot from the floor, and upon these were heaps of fruits. Some I recognized as a kind of hypertrophied raspberry and orange, but for the most part they were strange.

'Between the tables was scattered a great number of cushions. Upon these my conductors seated themselves, signing for me to do likewise. With a pretty absence of ceremony they began to eat the fruit with their hands, flinging peel and stalks and so forth, into the round openings in the sides of the tables. I was not loth to follow their example, for I felt thirsty and hungry. As I did so I surveyed the hall at my leisure.

'And perhaps the thing that struck me most was its dilapidated look. The stained-glass windows, which displayed only a geometrical pattern, were broken in many places, and the curtains that hung across the lower end were thick with dust. And it caught my eye that the corner of the marble table near me was fractured. Nevertheless, the general effect was extremely rich and picturesque. There were, perhaps, a couple of hundred people dining in the hall, and most of them, seated as near to me as they could come, were watching me with interest, their little eyes shining over the fruit they were eating. All were clad in the same soft, and yet strong, silky material.

'Fruit, by the bye, was all their diet. These people of the remote future were strict vegetarians, and while I was with them, in spite of some carnal cravings, I had to be frugivorous also. Indeed, I found afterwards that horses, cattle, sheep, dogs, had followed the Ichthyosaurus[2] into extinction. But the fruits were very delightful; one, in particular, that seemed to be in season all the time I was there – a floury thing in a three-sided husk – was especially good, and I made it my staple. At first I was puzzled by all these strange fruits, and by the strange flowers I saw, but later I began to perceive their import.

'However, I am telling you of my fruit dinner in the distant future now. So soon as my appetite was a little checked, I determined to make a resolute attempt to learn the speech of these new men of mine. Clearly that was the next thing to do. The fruits seemed a convenient thing to begin upon, and holding one of these up I began a series of interrogative sounds and gestures. I had some considerable difficulty in conveying my meaning. At first my efforts met with a stare of surprise or

inextinguishable laughter, but presently a fair-haired little creature seemed to grasp my intention and repeated a name. They
had to chatter and explain the business at great length to each
other, and my first attempts to make the exquisite little sounds
of their language caused an immense amount of amusement.
However, I felt like a schoolmaster amidst children, and per-
sisted, and presently I had a score of noun substantives at least
at my command; and then I got to demonstrative pronouns,
and even the verb "to eat". But it was slow work, and the little
people soon tired and wanted to get away from my interroga-
tions, so I determined, rather of necessity, to let them give their
lessons in little doses when they felt inclined. And very little
doses I found they were before long, for I never met people
more indolent or more easily fatigued.

'A queer thing I soon discovered about my little hosts, and
that was their lack of interest. They would come to me with
eager cries of astonishment, like children, but like children they
would soon stop examining me and wander away after some
other toy. The dinner and my conversational beginnings ended,
I noted for the first time that almost all those who had surrounded me at first were gone. It is odd, too, how speedily I
came to disregard these little people. I went out through the
portal into the sunlit world again so soon as my hunger was
satisfied. I was continually meeting more of these men of the
future, who would follow me a little distance, chatter and laugh
about me, and, having smiled and gesticulated in a friendly
way, leave me again to my own devices.

'The calm of evening was upon the world as I emerged from
the great hall, and the scene was lit by the warm glow of the
setting sun. At first things were very confusing. Everything was
so entirely different from the world I had known – even the
flowers. The big building I had left was situated on the slope of
a broad river valley, but the Thames had shifted, perhaps, a mile
from its present position. I resolved to mount to the summit of a
crest, perhaps a mile and a half away, from which I could get a
wider view of this our planet in the year Eight Hundred and Two
Thousand Seven Hundred and One A. D. For that, I should
explain, was the date the little dials of my machine recorded.

'As I walked I was watchful for every impression that could possibly help to explain the condition of ruinous splendour in which I found the world – for ruinous it was. A little way up the hill, for instance, was a great heap of granite, bound together by masses of aluminium, a vast labyrinth of precipitous walls and crumbled heaps, amidst which were thick heaps of very beautiful pagoda-like plants – nettles possibly – but wonderfully tinted with brown about the leaves, and incapable of stinging. It was evidently the derelict remains of some vast structure, to what end built I could not determine. It was here that I was destined, at a later date, to have a very strange experience – the first intimation of a still stranger discovery – but of that I will speak in its proper place.

'Looking round with a sudden thought, from a terrace on which I rested for a while, I realized that there were no small houses to be seen. Apparently the single house, and possibly even the household, had vanished. Here and there among the greenery were palace-like buildings, but the house and the cottage, which form such characteristic features of our own English landscape, had disappeared.

' "Communism," said I to myself.

'And on the heels of that came another thought. I looked at the half dozen little figures that were following me. Then, in a flash, I perceived that all had the same form of costume, the same soft hairless visage, and the same girlish rotundity of limb. It may seem strange, perhaps, that I had not noticed this before. But everything was so strange. Now, I saw the fact plainly enough. In costume, and in all the differences of texture and bearing that now mark off the sexes from each other, these people of the future were alike. And the children seemed to my eyes to be but the miniatures of their parents. I judged, then, that the children of that time were extremely precocious, physically at least, and I found afterwards abundant verification of my opinion.

'Seeing the ease and security in which these people were living, I felt that this close resemblance of the sexes was after all what one would expect; for the strength of a man and the softness of a woman, the institution of the family, and the differentiation of occupations are mere militant necessities of an age of physical force. Where population is balanced and abundant, much child-bearing becomes an evil rather than a blessing to the State; where violence comes but rarely and offspring are secure, there is less necessity – indeed there is no necessity – for an efficient family, and the specialization of the sexes[3] with reference to their children's needs disappears. We see some beginnings of this even in our own time, and in this future age it was complete. This, I must remind you, was my speculation at the time. Later, I was to appreciate how far it fell short of the reality.

'While I was musing upon these things, my attention was attracted by a pretty little structure, like a well under a cupola. I thought in a transitory way of the oddness of wells still existing, and then resumed the thread of my speculations. There were no large buildings towards the top of the hill, and as my walking powers were evidently miraculous, I was presently left alone for the first time. With a strange sense of freedom and adventure I pushed on up to the crest.

'There I found a seat of some yellow metal that I did not recognize, corroded in places with a kind of pinkish rust and half smothered in soft moss, the arm rests cast and filed into the resemblance of griffins' heads. I sat down on it, and I surveyed the broad view of our old world under the sunset of that long day. It was as sweet and fair a view as I have ever seen. The sun had already gone below the horizon and the west was flaming gold, touched with some horizontal bars of purple and crimson. Below was the valley of the Thames, in which the river lay like a band of burnished steel. I have already spoken of the great palaces dotted about among the variegated greenery, some in ruins and some still occupied. Here and there rose a white or silvery figure in the waste garden of the earth, here and there came the sharp vertical line of some cupola or obelisk. There were no hedges, no signs of proprietary rights, no evidences of agriculture; the whole earth had become a garden.

'So watching, I began to put my interpretation upon the things I had seen, and as it shaped itself to me that evening, my interpretation was something in this way. (Afterwards I found

I had got only a half-truth – or only a glimpse of one facet of the truth.)

'It seemed to me that I had happened upon humanity upon the wane. The ruddy sunset set me thinking of the sunset of mankind. For the first time I began to realize an odd consequence of the social effort in which we are at present engaged. And yet, come to think, it is a logical consequence enough. Strength is the outcome of need; security sets a premium on feebleness. The work of ameliorating the conditions of life – the true civilizing process that makes life more and more secure – had gone steadily on to a climax. One triumph of a united humanity over Nature had followed another. Things that are now mere dreams had become projects deliberately put in hand and carried forward. And the harvest was what I saw!

'After all, the sanitation and the agriculture of today are still in the rudimentary stage. The science of our time has attacked but a little department of the field of human disease, but, even so, it spreads its operations very steadily and persistently. Our agriculture and horticulture destroy a weed just here and there and cultivate perhaps a score or so of wholesome plants, leaving the greater number to fight out a balance as they can. We improve our favourite plants and animals – and how few they are – gradually by selective breeding; now a new and better peach, now a seedless grape, now a sweeter and larger flower, now a more convenient breed of cattle. We improve them gradually, because our ideals are vague and tentative, and our knowledge is very limited; because Nature, too, is shy and slow in our clumsy hands. Some day all this will be better organized, and still better. That is the drift of the current in spite of the eddies. The whole world will be intelligent, educated and cooperating; things will move faster and faster towards the subjugation of Nature. In the end, wisely and carefully we shall readjust the balance of animal and vegetable life to suit our human needs.

'This adjustment, I say, must have been done, and done well; done indeed for all time, in the space of Time across which my machine had leapt. The air was free from gnats, the earth from weeds or fungi; everywhere were fruits and sweet and delightful flowers; brilliant butterflies flew hither and thither. The ideal of preventive medicine was attained. Diseases had been stamped out. I saw no evidence of any contagious diseases during all my stay. And I shall have to tell you later that even the processes of putrefaction and decay had been profoundly affected by these changes.

'Social triumphs, too, had been effected. I saw mankind housed in splendid shelters, gloriously clothed, and as yet I had found them engaged in no toil. There were no signs of struggle, neither social nor economical struggle. The shop, the advertisement, traffic, all that commerce which constitutes the body of our world, was gone. It was natural on that golden evening that I should jump at the idea of a social paradise. The difficulty of increasing population had been met, I guessed, and population had ceased to increase.

'But with this change in condition comes inevitably adaptations to the change. What, unless biological science is a mass of errors, is the cause of human intelligence and vigour? Hardship and freedom: conditions under which the active, strong, and subtle survive and the weaker go to the wall; conditions that put a premium upon the loyal alliance of capable men, upon self-restraint, patience, and decision. And the institution of the family, and the emotions that arise therein, the fierce jealousy, the tenderness for offspring, parental self-devotion, all found their justification and support in the imminent dangers of the young. *Now*, where are these imminent dangers? There is a sentiment arising, and it will grow, against connubial jealousy, against fierce maternity, against passion of all sorts; unnecessary things now, and things that make us uncomfortable, savage survivals, discords in a refined and pleasant life.

'I thought of the physical slightness of the people, their lack of intelligence, and those big abundant ruins, and it strengthened my belief in a perfect conquest of Nature. For after the battle comes Quiet. Humanity had been strong, energetic and intelligent, and had used all its abundant vitality to alter the conditions under which it lived. And now came the reaction of the altered conditions.

'Under the new conditions of perfect comfort and security,

that restless energy, that with us is strength, would become weakness. Even in our own time certain tendencies and desires, once necessary to survival, are a constant source of failure. Physical courage and the love of battle, for instance, are no great help – may even be hindrances – to a civilized man. And in a state of physical balance and security, power, intellectual as well as physical, would be out of place. For countless years I judged there had been no danger of war or solitary violence, no danger from wild beasts, no wasting disease to require strength of constitution, no need of toil. For such a life, what we should call the weak are as well equipped as the strong, are indeed no longer weak. Better equipped indeed they are, for the strong would be fretted by an energy for which there was no outlet. No doubt the exquisite beauty of the buildings I saw was the outcome of the last surgings of the now purposeless energy of mankind before it settled down into perfect harmony with the conditions under which it lived – the flourish of that triumph which began the last great peace. This has ever been the fate of energy in security; it takes to art and to eroticism, and then come languor and decay.

'Even this artistic impetus would at last die away – had almost died in the Time I saw. To adorn themselves with flowers, to dance, to sing in the sunlight; so much was left of the artistic spirit, and no more. Even that would fade in the end into a contented inactivity. We are kept keen on the grindstone of pain and necessity, and, it seemed to me, that here was that hateful grindstone broken at last!

'As I stood there in the gathering dark I thought that in this simple explanation I had mastered the problem of the world – mastered the whole secret of these delicious people. Possibly the checks they had devised for the increase of population had succeeded too well, and their numbers had rather diminished than kept stationary. That would account for the abandoned ruins. Very simple was my explanation, and plausible enough – as most wrong theories are!

5

'As I stood there musing over this too perfect triumph of man, the full moon, yellow and gibbous,[1] came up out of an overflow of silver light in the north-east. The bright little figures ceased to move about below, a noiseless owl flitted by, and I shivered with the chill of the night. I determined to descend and find where I could sleep.

'I looked for the building I knew. Then my eye travelled along to the figure of the White Sphinx upon the pedestal of bronze, growing distinct as the light of the rising moon grew brighter. I could see the silver birch against it. There was the tangle of rhododendron bushes, black in the pale light, and there was the little lawn. I looked at the lawn again. A queer doubt chilled my complacency. "No," said I stoutly to myself, "that was not the lawn."

'But it *was* the lawn. For the white leprous face of the sphinx was towards it. Can you imagine what I felt as this conviction came home to me? But you cannot. The Time Machine was gone!

'At once, like a lash across the face, came the possibility of losing my own age, of being left helpless in this strange new world. The bare thought of it was an actual physical sensation. I could feel it grip me at the throat and stop my breathing. In another moment I was in a passion of fear and running with great leaping strides down the slope. Once I fell headlong and cut my face; I lost no time in stanching the blood, but jumped up and ran on, with a warm trickle down my cheek and chin. All the time I ran I was saying to myself, "They have moved it a little, pushed it under the bushes out of the way." Nevertheless, I ran with all my might. All the time, with the certainty that sometimes comes with excessive dread, I knew that such assurance was folly, knew instinctively that the machine was removed out of my reach. My breath came with pain. I suppose I covered the whole distance from the hill crest to the little lawn, two miles, perhaps, in ten minutes. And I am not a young man. I cursed aloud, as I ran, at my confident folly in leaving the machine, wasting good breath thereby. I cried aloud, and none answered. Not a creature seemed to be stirring in that moonlit world.

'When I reached the lawn my worst fears were realized. Not a trace of the thing was to be seen. I felt faint and cold when I faced the empty space among the black tangle of bushes. I ran round it furiously, as if the thing might be hidden in a corner, and then stopped abruptly, with my hands clutching my hair. Above me towered the sphinx, upon the bronze pedestal, white, shining, leprous, in the light of the rising moon. It seemed to smile in mockery of my dismay.

'I might have consoled myself by imagining the little people had put the mechanism in some shelter for me, had I not felt assured of their physical and intellectual inadequacy. That is what dismayed me: the sense of some hitherto unsuspected power, through whose intervention my invention had vanished. Yet, of one thing I felt assured: unless some other age had produced its exact duplicate, the machine could not have moved in time. The attachment of the levers – I will show you the method later – prevented anyone from tampering with it in that way when they were removed. It had moved, and was hid, only in space. But then, where could it be?

'I think I must have had a kind of frenzy. I remember running violently in and out among the moonlit bushes all round the sphinx, and startling some white animal that, in the dim light, I took for a small deer. I remember, too, late that night, beating the bushes with my clenched fists until my knuckles were gashed and bleeding from the broken twigs. Then, sobbing and raving in my anguish of mind, I went down to the great building of stone. The big hall was dark, silent and deserted. I slipped on the uneven floor, and fell over one of the malachite tables, almost breaking my shin. I lit a match and went on past the dusty curtains, of which I have told you.

'There I found a second great hall covered with cushions, upon which, perhaps, a score or so of the little people were sleeping. I have no doubt they found my second appearance strange enough, coming suddenly out of the quiet darkness with inarticulate noises and the splutter and flare of a match. For they had forgotten about matches. "Where is my Time Machine?" I began, bawling like an angry child, laying hands upon them and shaking them up together. It must have been very queer to them. Some laughed, most of them looked sorely frightened. When I saw them standing round me, it came into my head that I was doing as foolish a thing as it was possible for me to do under the circumstances, in trying to revive the sensation of fear. For, reasoning from their daylight behaviour, I thought that fear must be forgotten.

'Abruptly, I dashed down the match, and, knocking one of the people over in my course, went blundering across the big dining-hall again, out under the moonlight. I heard cries of terror and their little feet running and stumbling this way and that. I do not remember all I did as the moon crept up the sky. I suppose it was the unexpected nature of my loss that maddened me. I felt hopelessly cut off from my own kind – a strange animal in an unknown world. I must have raved to and fro, screaming and crying upon God and Fate. I have a memory of horrible fatigue, as the long night of despair wore away; of looking in this impossible place and that; of groping among moonlit ruins and touching strange creatures in the black shadows; at last, of lying on the ground near the sphinx and weeping with absolute wretchedness. I had nothing left but misery. Then I slept, and when I woke again it was full day, and a couple of sparrows were hopping round me on the turf within reach of my arm.

'I sat up in the freshness of the morning, trying to remember how I had got there, and why I had such a profound sense of desertion and despair. Then things came clear in my mind. With the plain, reasonable daylight, I could look my circumstances fairly in the face. I saw the wild folly of my frenzy overnight, and I could reason with myself. Suppose the worst? I said. Suppose the machine altogether lost – perhaps destroyed? It behoves me to be calm and patient, to learn the way of the people, to get a clear idea of the method of my loss, and the means of getting materials and tools; so that in the end, perhaps, I may make another. That would be my only hope, a poor hope perhaps, but better than despair. And, after all, it was a beautiful and curious world.

'But probably the machine had only been taken away. Still, I must be calm and patient, find its hiding-place, and recover it by force or cunning. And with that I scrambled to my feet and looked about me, wondering where I could bathe. I felt weary, stiff and travel-soiled. The freshness of the morning made me desire an equal freshness. I had exhausted my emotion. Indeed, as I went about my business, I found myself wondering at my intense excitement overnight. I made a careful examination of the ground about the little lawn. I wasted some time in futile questionings, conveyed, as well as I was able, to such of the little people as came by. They all failed to understand my gestures; some were simply stolid, some thought it was a jest and laughed at me. I had the hardest task in the world to keep my hands off their pretty laughing faces. It was a foolish impulse, but the devil begotten of fear and blind anger was ill curbed and still eager to take advantage of my perplexity. The turf gave better counsel. I found a groove ripped in it, about midway between the pedestal of the sphinx and the marks of my feet where, on arrival, I had struggled with the overturned machine. There were other signs of removal about, with queer narrow footprints like those I could imagine made by a sloth. This directed my closer attention to the pedestal. It was, as I think I have said, of bronze. It was not a mere block, but highly decorated with deep framed panels on either side. I went and rapped at these. The pedestal was hollow. Examining the panels with care I found them discontinuous with the frames. There were no handles or keyholes, but possibly the panels, if they were doors, as I supposed, opened from within. One thing was clear enough to my mind. It took no very great mental effort to infer that my Time Machine was inside that pedestal. But how it got there was a different problem.

'I saw the heads of two orange-clad people coming through the bushes and under some blossom-covered apple trees towards me. I turned smiling to them and beckoned them to me. They came, and then, pointing to the bronze pedestal, I tried to intimate my wish to open it. But at my first gesture towards this they behaved very oddly. I don't know how to convey their expression to you. Suppose you were to use a grossly improper gesture to a delicate-minded woman – it is how she would look. They went off as if they had received the last possible insult. I tried a sweet-looking little chap in white next, with exactly the same result. Somehow, his manner made me feel ashamed of myself. But, as you know, I wanted the Time Machine, and I tried him once more. As he turned off, like the others, my temper got the better of me. In three strides I was after him, had him by the loose part of his robe round the neck, and began dragging him towards the sphinx. Then I saw the horror and repugnance of his face, and all of a sudden I let him go.

'But I was not beaten yet. I banged with my fist at the bronze panels. I thought I heard something stir inside – to be explicit, I thought I heard a sound like a chuckle – but I must have been mistaken. Then I got a big pebble from the river, and came and hammered till I had flattened a coil in the decorations, and the verdigris came off in powdery flakes. The delicate little people must have heard me hammering in gusty outbreaks a mile away on either hand, but nothing came of it. I saw a crowd of them upon the slopes, looking furtively at me. At last, hot and tired, I sat down to watch the place. But I was too restless to watch long; I am too Occidental for a long vigil. I could work at a problem for years, but to wait inactive for twenty-four hours – that is another matter.

'I got up after a time, and began walking aimlessly through the bushes towards the hill again. "Patience," said I to myself. "If you want your machine again you must leave that sphinx alone. If they mean to take your machine away, it's little good your wrecking their bronze panels, and if they don't, you will get it back as soon as you can ask for it. To sit among all those unknown things before a puzzle like that is hopeless. That way lies monomania.[2] Face this world. Learn its ways, watch it, be careful of too hasty guesses at its meaning. In the end you will find clues to it all." Then suddenly the humour of the situation came into my mind: the thought of the years I had spent in study and toil to get into the future age, and now my passion of anxiety to get out of it. I had made myself the most complicated and the most hopeless trap that ever a man devised. Although it was at my own expense, I could not help myself. I laughed aloud.

'Going through the big palace, it seemed to me that the little people avoided me. It may have been my fancy, or it may have had something to do with my hammering at the gates of bronze. Yet I felt tolerably sure of the avoidance. I was careful, however, to show no concern and to abstain from any pursuit of them, and in the course of a day or two things got back to the old footing. I made what progress I could in the language, and in addition I pushed my explorations here and there. Either I missed some subtle point, or their language was excessively simple – almost exclusively composed of concrete substantives and verbs. There seemed to be few, if any, abstract terms, or little use of figurative language. Their sentences were usually simple and of two words, and I failed to convey or understand any but the simplest propositions. I determined to put the thought of my Time Machine and the mystery of the bronze doors under the sphinx as much as possible in a corner of memory, until my growing knowledge would lead me back to them in a natural way. Yet a certain feeling, you may understand, tethered me in a circle of a few miles round the point of my arrival.

'So far as I could see, all the world displayed the same exuberant richness as the Thames valley. From every hill I climbed I saw the same abundance of splendid buildings, endlessly varied in material and style, the same clustering thickets of evergreens, the same blossom-laden trees and tree-ferns. Here and there water shone like silver, and beyond, the land rose into blue undulating hills, and so faded into the serenity of the sky. A peculiar feature, which presently attracted my attention, was the presence of certain circular wells, several, as it seemed to me, of a very great depth. One lay by the path up the hill, which I had followed during my first walk. Like the others, it was rimmed with bronze, curiously wrought, and protected by a little cupola from the rain. Sitting by the side of these wells, and peering down into the shafted darkness, I could see no gleam of water, nor could I start any reflection with a lighted match. But in all of them I heard a certain sound: a thud–thud–thud, like the beating of some big engine; and I discovered, from the flaring of my matches, that a steady current of air set down the shafts. Further, I threw a scrap of paper into the throat of one, and, instead of fluttering slowly down, it was at once sucked swiftly out of sight.

'After a time, too, I came to connect these wells with tall towers standing here and there upon the slopes; for above them there was often just such a flicker in the air as one sees on a hot day above a sun-scorched beach. Putting things together, I reached a strong suggestion of an extensive system of subterranean ventilation, whose true import it was difficult to imagine. I was at first inclined to associate it with the sanitary apparatus of these people. It was an obvious conclusion, but it was absolutely wrong.

'And here I must admit that I learned very little of drains and bells and modes of conveyance, and the like conveniences, during my time in this real future. In some of these visions of Utopias and coming times which I have read, there is a vast amount of detail about building, and social arrangements, and so forth. But while such details are easy enough to obtain when the whole world is contained in one's imagination, they are altogether inaccessible to a real traveller amid such realities as I found here. Conceive the tale of London which a negro, fresh from Central Africa, would take back to his tribe! What would he know of railway companies, of social movements, of telephone and telegraph wires, of the Parcels Delivery Company, and postal orders and the like? Yet we, at least, should be willing enough to explain these things to him! And even of what he knew, how much could he make his untravelled friend either apprehend or believe? Then, think how narrow the gap between a negro and a white man of our own times, and how wide the interval between myself and these of the Golden Age! I was sensible of much which was unseen, and which contributed to my comfort; but save for a general impression of automatic organization, I fear I can convey very little of the difference to your mind.

'In the matter of sepulture, for instance, I could see no signs of crematoria nor anything suggestive of tombs. But it occurred to me that, possibly, there might be cemeteries (or crematoria) somewhere beyond the range of my explorings. This, again, was a question I deliberately put to myself, and my curiosity was at first entirely defeated upon the point. The thing puzzled me, and I was led to make a further remark, which puzzled me still more: that aged and infirm among this people there were none.

'I must confess that my satisfaction with my first theories of an automatic civilization and a decadent humanity did not long endure. Yet I could think of no other. Let me put my difficulties. The several big palaces I had explored were mere living places, great dining-halls and sleeping apartments. I could find no machinery, no appliances of any kind. Yet these people were clothed in pleasant fabrics that must at times need renewal, and their sandals, though undecorated, were fairly complex specimens of metalwork. Somehow such things must be made. And the little people displayed no vestige of a creative tendency. There were no shops, no workshops, no sign of importations among them. They spent all their time in playing gently, in bathing in the river, in making love in a half-playful fashion, in eating fruit and sleeping. I could not see how things were kept going.

'Then, again, about the Time Machine: something, I knew not what, had taken it into the hollow pedestal of the White Sphinx. *Why?* For the life of me I could not imagine. Those waterless wells, too, those flickering pillars. I felt I lacked a clue. I felt – how shall I put it? Suppose you found an inscription, with sentences here and there in excellent plain English, and, interpolated therewith, others made up of words, of letters

even, absolutely unknown to you? Well, on the third day of my
visit, that was how the world of Eight Hundred and Two
Thousand Seven Hundred and One presented itself to me!

'That day, too, I made a friend – of a sort. It happened that,
as I was watching some of the little people bathing in a shallow,
one of them was seized with cramp and began drifting down-
stream. The main current ran rather swiftly, but not too
strongly for even a moderate swimmer. It will give you an idea,
therefore, of the strange deficiency in these creatures, when I
tell you that none made the slightest attempt to rescue the
weakly crying little thing which was drowning before their eyes.
When I realized this, I hurriedly slipped off my clothes, and,
wading in at a point lower down, I caught the poor mite and
drew her safe to land. A little rubbing of the limbs soon brought
her round, and I had the satisfaction of seeing she was all
right before I left her. I had got to such a low estimate of her
kind that I did not expect any gratitude from her. In that,
however, I was wrong.

'This happened in the morning. In the afternoon I met my
little woman, as I believe it was, as I was returning towards my
centre from an exploration, and she received me with cries of
delight and presented me with a big garland of flowers – evidently made for me and me alone. The thing took my imagination. Very possibly I had been feeling desolate. At any rate I did
my best to display my appreciation of the gift. We were soon
seated together in a little stone arbour, engaged in conversation,
chiefly of smiles. The creature's friendliness affected me exactly
as a child's might have done. We passed each other flowers,
and she kissed my hands. I did the same to hers. Then I tried
talk, and found that her name was Weena,[3] which, though I
don't know what it meant, somehow seemed appropriate
enough. That was the beginning of a queer friendship which
lasted a week, and ended – as I will tell you!

'She was exactly like a child. She wanted to be with me
always. She tried to follow me everywhere, and on my next
journey out and about it went to my heart to tire her down,
and leave her at last, exhausted and calling after me rather
plaintively. But the problems of the world had to be mastered.

I had not, I said to myself, come into the future to carry on a miniature flirtation. Yet her distress when I left her was very great, her expostulations at the parting were sometimes frantic, and I think, altogether, I had as much trouble as comfort from her devotion. Nevertheless she was, somehow, a very great comfort. I thought it was mere childish affection that made her cling to me. Until it was too late, I did not clearly know what I had inflicted upon her when I left her. Nor until it was too late did I clearly understand what she was to me. For, by merely seeming fond of me, and showing in her weak, futile way that she cared for me, the little doll of a creature presently gave my return to the neighbourhood of the White Sphinx almost the feeling of coming home; and I would watch for her tiny figure of white and gold so soon as I came over the hill.

'It was from her, too, that I learned that fear had not yet left the world. She was fearless enough in the daylight, and she had the oddest confidence in me; for once, in a foolish moment, I made threatening grimaces at her, and she simply laughed at them. But she dreaded the dark, dreaded shadows, dreaded black things. Darkness to her was the one thing dreadful. It was a singularly passionate emotion, and it set me thinking and observing. I discovered then, among other things, that these little people gathered into the great houses after dark, and slept in droves. To enter upon them without a light was to put them into a tumult of apprehension. I never found one out of doors, or one sleeping alone within doors, after dark. Yet I was still such a blockhead that I missed the lesson of that fear, and in spite of Weena's distress, I insisted upon sleeping away from these slumbering multitudes.

'It troubled her greatly, but in the end her odd affection for me triumphed, and for five of the nights of our acquaintance, including the last night of all, she slept with her head pillowed on my arm. But my story slips away from me as I speak of her. It must have been the night before her rescue that I was awakened about dawn. I had been restless, dreaming most disagreeably that I was drowned, and that sea-anemones were feeling over my face with their soft palps. I woke with a start, and with an odd fancy that some greyish animal had just rushed out of the chamber. I tried to get to sleep again, but I felt restless and uncomfortable. It was that dim grey hour when things are just creeping out of darkness, when everything is colourless and clear cut, and yet unreal. I got up, and went down into the great hall, and so out upon the flagstones in front of the palace. I thought I would make a virtue of necessity, and see the sunrise.

'The moon was setting, and the dying moonlight and the first pallor of dawn were mingled in a ghastly half-light. The bushes were inky black, the ground a sombre grey, the sky colourless and cheerless. And up the hill I thought I could see ghosts. Three several times, as I scanned the slope, I saw white figures. Twice I fancied I saw a solitary white, ape-like creature running rather quickly up the hill, and once near the ruins I saw a leash of them carrying some dark body. They moved hastily. I did not see what became of them. It seemed that they vanished among the bushes. The dawn was still indistinct, you must understand. I was feeling that chill, uncertain, early-morning feeling you may have known. I doubted my eyes.

'As the eastern sky grew brighter, and the light of the day came on and its vivid colouring returned upon the world once more, I scanned the view keenly. But I saw no vestige of my white figures. They were mere creatures of the half-light. "They must have been ghosts," I said; "I wonder whence they dated." For a queer notion of Grant Allen's[4] came into my head, and amused me. If each generation die and leave ghosts, he argued, the world at last will get overcrowded with them. On that theory they would have grown innumerable some Eight Hundred Thousand Years hence, and it was no great wonder to see four at once. But the jest was unsatisfying, and I was thinking of these figures all the morning, until Weena's rescue drove them out of my head. I associated them in some indefinite way with the white animal I had startled in my first passionate search for the Time Machine. But Weena was a pleasant substitute. Yet all the same, they were soon destined to take far deadlier possession of my mind.

'I think I have said how much hotter than our own was the weather of this Golden Age. I cannot account for it. It may be that the sun was hotter, or the earth nearer the sun. It is usual to assume that the sun will go on cooling steadily in the future. But people, unfamiliar with such speculations as those of the younger Darwin, forget that the planets must ultimately fall back one by one into the parent body.[5] As these catastrophes occur, the sun will blaze with renewed energy; and it may be that some inner planet had suffered this fate. Whatever the reason, the fact remains that the sun was very much hotter than we know it.

'Well, one very hot morning – my fourth, I think – as I was seeking shelter from the heat and glare in a colossal ruin near the great house where I slept and fed, there happened this strange thing: Clambering among these heaps of masonry, I found a narrow gallery, whose end and side windows were blocked by fallen masses of stone. By contrast with the brilliancy outside, it seemed at first impenetrably dark to me. I entered it groping, for the change from light to blackness made spots of colour swim before me. Suddenly I halted spellbound. A pair of eyes, luminous by reflection against the daylight without, was watching me out of the darkness.

'The old instinctive dread of wild beasts came upon me. I clenched my hands and steadfastly looked into the glaring eyeballs. I was afraid to turn. Then the thought of the absolute security in which humanity appeared to be living came to my mind. And then I remembered that strange terror of the dark. Overcoming my fear to some extent, I advanced a step and spoke. I will admit that my voice was harsh and ill-controlled. I put out my hand and touched something soft. At once the eyes darted sideways, and something white ran past me. I turned with my heart in my mouth, and saw a queer little ape-like figure, its head held down in a peculiar manner, running across the sunlit space behind me. It blundered against a block of granite, staggered aside, and in a moment was hidden in a black shadow beneath another pile of ruined masonry.

'My impression of it is, of course, imperfect; but I know it was a dull white, and had strange large greyish-red eyes; also that there was flaxen hair on its head and down its back. But, as I say, it went too fast for me to see distinctly. I cannot even

say whether it ran on all fours, or only with its forearms held
very low. After an instant's pause I followed it into the second
heap of ruins. I could not find it at first; but, after a time in the
profound obscurity, I came upon one of those round well-like
openings of which I have told you, half closed by a fallen pillar.
A sudden thought came to me. Could this Thing have vanished
down the shaft? I lit a match, and, looking down, I saw a small,
white, moving creature, with large bright eyes which regarded
me steadfastly as it retreated. It made me shudder. It was so
like a human spider! It was clambering down the wall, and now
I saw for the first time a number of metal foot and hand rests
forming a kind of ladder down the shaft. Then the light burned
my fingers and fell out of my hand, going out as it dropped,
and when I had lit another the little monster had disappeared.

'I do not know how long I sat peering down that well. It was
not for some time that I could succeed in persuading myself
that the thing I had seen was human. But, gradually, the truth
dawned on me: that Man had not remained one species, but
had differentiated into two distinct animals: that my graceful
children of the Upperworld were not the sole descendants of
our generation, but that this bleached, obscene, nocturnal
Thing, which had flashed before me, was also heir to all the ages.

'I thought of the flickering pillars and of my theory of an
underground ventilation. I began to suspect their true import.
And what, I wondered, was this Lemur[6] doing in my scheme of
a perfectly balanced organization? How was it related to the
indolent serenity of the beautiful Upperworlders? And what
was hidden down there, at the foot of that shaft? I sat upon the
edge of the well telling myself that, at any rate, there was
nothing to fear, and that there I must descend for the solution
of my difficulties. And withal I was absolutely afraid to go!
As I hesitated, two of the beautiful Upperworld people came
running in their amorous sport across the daylight into the
shadow. The male pursued the female, flinging flowers at her
as he ran.

'They seemed distressed to find me, my arm against the overturned pillar, peering down the well. Apparently it was con-
sidered bad form to remark these apertures; for when I pointed

to this one, and tried to frame a question about it in their tongue, they were still more visibly distressed and turned away. But they were interested by my matches, and I struck some to amuse them. I tried them again about the well, and again I failed. So presently I left them, meaning to go back to Weena, and see what I could get from her. But my mind was already in revolution; my guesses and impressions were slipping and sliding to a new adjustment. I had now a clue to the import of these wells, to the ventilating towers, to the mystery of the ghosts; to say nothing of a hint at the meaning of the bronze gates and the fate of the Time Machine! And very vaguely there came a suggestion towards the solution of the economic problem that had puzzled me.

'Here was the new view. Plainly, this second species of Man was subterranean. There were three circumstances in particular which made me think that its rare emergence above ground was the outcome of a long-continued underground habit. In the first place, there was the bleached look common in most animals that live largely in the dark – the white fish of the Kentucky caves, for instance. Then, those large eyes, with that capacity for reflecting light, are common features of nocturnal things – witness the owl and the cat. And last of all, that evident confusion in the sunshine, that hasty yet fumbling and awkward flight towards dark shadow, and that peculiar carriage of the head while in the light – all reinforced the theory of an extreme sensitiveness of the retina.

'Beneath my feet, then, the earth must be tunnelled enormously, and these tunnellings were the habitat of the new race. The presence of ventilating-shafts and wells along the hill slopes – everywhere, in fact, except along the river valley – showed how universal were its ramifications. What so natural, then, as to assume that it was in this artificial Underworld that such work as was necessary to the comfort of the daylight race was done? The notion was so plausible that I at once accepted it, and went on to assume the *how* of this splitting of the human species. I dare say you will anticipate the shape of my theory; though, for myself, I very soon felt that it fell far short of the truth.

'At first, proceeding from the problems of our own age, it seemed clear as daylight to me that the gradual widening of the present merely temporary and social difference between the Capitalist and the Labourer, was the key to the whole position. No doubt it will seem grotesque enough to you – and wildly incredible! – and yet even now there are existing circumstances to point that way. There is a tendency to utilize underground space for the less ornamental purposes of civilization; there is the Metropolitan Railway in London,[7] for instance, there are new electric railways, there are subways, there are underground workrooms and restaurants, and they increase and multiply. Evidently, I thought, this tendency had increased till industry had gradually lost its birthright in the sky. I mean that it had gone deeper and deeper into larger and ever larger underground factories, spending a still-increasing amount of its time therein, till, in the end –! Even now, does not an East-end worker live in such artificial conditions as practically to be cut off from the natural surface of the earth?[8]

'Again, the exclusive tendency of richer people – due, no doubt, to the increasing refinement of their education, and the widening gulf between them and the rude violence of the poor – is already leading to the closing, in their interest, of considerable portions of the surface of the land. About London, for instance, perhaps half the prettier country is shut in against intrusion. And this same widening gulf – which is due to the length and expense of the higher educational process and the increased facilities for and temptations towards refined habits on the part of the rich – will make that exchange between class and class, that promotion by intermarriage which at present retards the splitting of our species along lines of social stratification, less and less frequent.[9] So, in the end, above ground you must have the Haves, pursuing pleasure and comfort and beauty, and below ground the Have-nots, the Workers getting continually adapted to the conditions of their labour. Once they were there, they would no doubt have to pay rent, and not a little of it, for the ventilation of their caverns; and if they refused, they would starve or be suffocated for arrears. Such of them as were so constituted as to be miserable and rebellious would die; and, in the end, the balance being permanent, the survivors would become as well adapted to the conditions of underground life, and as happy in their way, as the Upperworld people were to theirs. As it seemed to me, the refined beauty and the etiolated pallor followed naturally enough.

'The great triumph of Humanity I had dreamed of took a different shape in my mind. It had been no such triumph of moral education and general cooperation as I had imagined. Instead, I saw a real aristocracy, armed with a perfected science and working to a logical conclusion the industrial system of today. Its triumph had not been simply a triumph over Nature, but a triumph over Nature and the fellow man. This, I must warn you, was my theory at the time. I had no convenient cicerone in the pattern of the Utopian books.[10] My explanation may be absolutely wrong. I still think it is the most plausible one. But even on this supposition the balanced civilization that was at last attained must have long since passed its zenith, and was now far fallen into decay. The too-perfect security of the Upperworlders had led them to a slow movement of degeneration, to a general dwindling in size, strength and intelligence.[11] That I could see clearly enough already. What had happened to the Undergrounders I did not yet suspect; but, from what I had seen of the Morlocks – that, by the bye, was the name by which these creatures were called – I could imagine that the modification of the human type was even far more profound than among the "Eloi",[12] the beautiful race that I already knew.

'Then came troublesome doubts. Why had the Morlocks taken my Time Machine? For I felt sure it was they who had taken it. Why, too, if the Eloi were masters, could they not restore the machine to me? And why were they so terribly afraid of the dark? I proceeded, as I have said, to question Weena about this Underworld, but here again I was disappointed. At first she would not understand my questions, and presently she refused to answer them. She shivered as though the topic was unendurable. And when I pressed her, perhaps a little harshly, she burst into tears. They were the only tears, except my own, I ever saw in that Golden Age. When I saw them I ceased abruptly to trouble about the Morlocks, and was only concerned in banishing these signs of the human inheritance from Weena's eyes. And very soon she was smiling and clapping her hands while I solemnly burnt a match.

6

'It may seem odd to you, but it was two days before I could follow up the new-found clue in what was manifestly the proper way. I felt a peculiar shrinking from those pallid bodies. They were just the half-bleached colour of the worms and things one sees preserved in spirit in a zoological museum. And they were filthily cold to the touch. Probably my shrinking was largely due to the sympathetic influence of the Eloi, whose disgust of the Morlocks I now began to appreciate.

'The next night I did not sleep well. Probably my health was a little disordered. I was oppressed with perplexity and doubt. Once or twice I had a feeling of intense fear for which I could perceive no definite reason. I remember creeping noiselessly into the great hall where the little people were sleeping in the moonlight – that night Weena was among them – and feeling reassured by their presence. It occurred to me, even then, that in the course of a few days the moon must pass through its last quarter, and the nights grow dark, when the appearances of these unpleasant creatures from below, these whitened Lemurs, this new vermin that had replaced the old, might be more abundant. And on both these days I had the restless feeling of one who shirks an inevitable duty. I felt assured that the Time Machine was only to be recovered by boldly penetrating these underground mysteries. Yet I could not face the mystery. If only I had had a companion it would have been different. But I was so horribly alone, and even to clamber down into the darkness of the well appalled me. I don't know if you will understand my feeling, but I never felt quite safe at my back.

'It was this restlessness, this insecurity, perhaps, that drove me further and further afield in my exploring expeditions. Going to the south-westward towards the rising country that is now called Combe Wood, I observed far off, in the direction of nineteenth-century Banstead, a vast green structure, different in character from any I had hitherto seen. It was larger than the largest of the palaces or ruins I knew, and the façade had an Oriental look: the face of it having the lustre, as well as the pale-green tint, a kind of bluish-green, of a certain type of Chinese porcelain. This difference in aspect suggested a difference in use, and I was minded to push on and explore. But the day was growing late, and I had come upon the sight of the place after a long and tiring circuit; so I resolved to hold over the adventure for the following day, and I returned to the welcome and the caresses of little Weena. But next morning I perceived clearly enough that my curiosity regarding the Palace of Green Porcelain was a piece of self-deception, to enable me to shirk, by another day, an experience I dreaded. I resolved I would make the descent without further waste of time, and started out in the early morning towards a well near the ruins of granite and aluminium.

'Little Weena ran with me. She danced beside me to the well, but when she saw me lean over the mouth and look downward, she seemed strangely disconcerted. "Goodbye, little Weena," I said, kissing her; and then, putting her down, I began to feel over the parapet for the climbing hooks. Rather hastily, I may as well confess, for I feared my courage might leak away! At first she watched me in amazement. Then she gave a most piteous cry, and, running to me, she began to pull at me with her little hands. I think her opposition nerved me rather to proceed. I shook her off, perhaps a little roughly, and in another moment I was in the throat of the well. I saw her agonized face over the parapet, and smiled to reassure her. Then I had to look down at the unstable hooks to which I clung.

'I had to clamber down a shaft of perhaps two hundred yards. The descent was effected by means of metallic bars projecting from the sides of the well, and these being adapted to the needs of a creature much smaller and lighter than myself, I was speedily cramped and fatigued by the descent. And not simply fatigued! One of the bars bent suddenly under my weight, and almost swung me off into the blackness beneath. For a moment I hung by one hand, and after that experience I did not dare to rest again. Though my arms and back were presently acutely painful, I went on clambering down the sheer descent with as quick a motion as possible. Glancing upward, I saw the aperture, a small blue disk, in which a star was visible, while little Weena's head showed as a round black projection. The thudding sound of a machine below grew louder and more oppressive. Everything save that little disk above was profoundly dark, and when I looked up again Weena had disappeared.

'I was in an agony of discomfort. I had some thought of trying to go up the shaft again, and leave the Underworld alone. But even while I turned this over in my mind I continued to descend. At last, with intense relief, I saw dimly coming up, a foot to the right of me, a slender loophole in the wall. Swinging myself in, I found it was the aperture of a narrow horizontal tunnel in which I could lie down and rest. It was not too soon. My arms ached, my back was cramped, and I was trembling with the prolonged terror of a fall. Besides this, the unbroken darkness had had a distressing effect upon my eyes. The air was full of the throb and hum of machinery pumping air down the shaft.

'I do not know how long I lay. I was roused by a soft hand touching my face. Starting up in the darkness I snatched at my matches and, hastily striking one, I saw three stooping white creatures similar to the one I had seen above ground in the ruin, hastily retreating before the light. Living, as they did, in what appeared to me impenetrable darkness, their eyes were abnormally large and sensitive, just as are the pupils of the abysmal fishes, and they reflected the light in the same way. I have no doubt they could see me in that rayless obscurity, and they did not seem to have any fear of me apart from the light. But, so soon as I struck a match in order to see them, they fled incontinently, vanishing into dark gutters and tunnels, from which their eyes glared at me in the strangest fashion.

'I tried to call to them, but the language they had was apparently different from that of the Upperworld people; so that I was needs left to my own unaided efforts, and the thought of flight before exploration was even then in my mind. But I said to myself, "You are in for it now," and, feeling my way along the tunnel, I found the noise of machinery grow louder. Presently the walls fell away from me, and I came to a large open space, and, striking another match, saw that I had entered a vast arched cavern, which stretched into utter darkness beyond the range of my light. The view I had of it was as much as one could see in the burning of a match.

'Necessarily my memory is vague. Great shapes like big machines rose out of the dimness, and cast grotesque black shadows, in which dim spectral Morlocks sheltered from the glare. The place, by the bye, was very stuffy and oppressive, and the faint halitus[1] of freshly shed blood was in the air. Some way down the central vista was a little table of white metal, laid with what seemed a meal. The Morlocks at any rate were carnivorous! Even at the time, I remember wondering what large animal could have survived to furnish the red joint I saw. It was all very indistinct: the heavy smell, the big unmeaning shapes, the obscene figures lurking in the shadows, and only waiting for the darkness to come at me again! Then the match burnt down, and stung my fingers, and fell, a wriggling red spot in the blackness.

'I have thought since how particularly ill equipped I was for such an experience. When I had started with the Time Machine, I had started with the absurd assumption that the men of the Future would certainly be infinitely ahead of ourselves in all their appliances. I had come without arms, without medicine, without anything to smoke – at times I missed tobacco frightfully! – even without enough matches. If only I had thought of a Kodak![2] I could have flashed that glimpse of the Underworld in a second, and examined it at leisure. But, as it was, I stood there with only the weapons and the powers that Nature had endowed me with – hands, feet and teeth; these, and four safety-matches that still remained to me.

'I was afraid to push my way in among all this machinery in

the dark, and it was only with my last glimpse of light I discovered that my store of matches had run low. It had never occurred to me until that moment that there was any need to economize them, and I had wasted almost half the box in astonishing the Upperworlders, to whom fire was a novelty. Now, as I say, I had four left, and while I stood in the dark, a hand touched mine, lank fingers came feeling over my face, and I was sensible of a peculiar unpleasant odour. I fancied I heard the breathing of a crowd of those dreadful little beings about me. I felt the box of matches in my hand being gently disengaged, and other hands behind me plucking at my clothing. The sense of these unseen creatures examining me was indescribably unpleasant. The sudden realization of my ignorance of their ways of thinking and doing came home to me very vividly in the darkness. I shouted at them as loudly as I could. They started away, and then I could feel them approaching me again. They clutched at me more boldly, whispering odd sounds to each other. I shivered violently, and shouted again – rather discordantly. This time they were not so seriously alarmed, and they made a queer laughing noise as they came back at me. I will confess I was horribly frightened. I determined to strike another match and escape under the protection of its glare. I did so, and eking out the flicker with a scrap of paper from my pocket, I made good my retreat to the narrow tunnel. But I had scarce entered this when my light was blown out, and in the blackness I could hear the Morlocks rustling like wind among leaves, and pattering like the rain, as they hurried after me.

'In a moment I was clutched by several hands, and there was no mistaking that they were trying to haul me back. I struck another light, and waved it in their dazzled faces. You can scarce imagine how nauseatingly inhuman they looked – those pale, chinless faces and great, lidless, pinkish-grey eyes! – as they started in their blindness and bewilderment. But I did not stay to look, I promise you: I retreated again, and when my second match had ended, I struck my third. It had almost burnt through when I reached the opening into the shaft. I lay down on the edge, for the throb of the great pump below made me giddy. Then I felt sideways for the projecting hooks, and, as I did so, my feet were grasped from behind, and I was violently tugged backward. I lit my last match . . . and it incontinently went out. But I had my hand on the climbing bars now, and, kicking violently, I disengaged myself from the clutches of the Morlocks, and was speedily clambering up the shaft, while they stayed peering and blinking up at me: all but one little wretch who followed me for some way, and well-nigh secured my boot as a trophy.

'That climb seemed interminable to me. With the last twenty or thirty feet of it a deadly nausea came upon me. I had the greatest difficulty in keeping my hold. The last few yards was a frightful struggle against this faintness. Several times my head swam, and I felt all the sensations of falling. At last, however, I got over the well-mouth somehow, and staggered out of the ruin into the blinding sunlight. I fell upon my face. Even the soil smelt sweet and clean. Then I remember Weena kissing my hands and ears, and the voices of others among the Eloi. Then, for a time, I was insensible.

7

'Now, indeed, I seemed in a worse case than before. Hitherto, except during my night's anguish at the loss of the Time Machine, I had felt a sustaining hope of ultimate escape, but that hope was staggered by these new discoveries. Hitherto I had merely thought myself impeded by the childish simplicity of the little people, and by some unknown forces which I had only to understand to overcome; but there was an altogether new element in the sickening quality of the Morlocks – a something inhuman and malign. Instinctively I loathed them. Before, I had felt as a man might feel who had fallen into a pit: my concern was with the pit and how to get out of it. Now I felt like a beast in a trap, whose enemy would come upon him soon.

'The enemy I dreaded may surprise you. It was the darkness of the new moon. Weena had put this into my head by some at first incomprehensible remarks about the Dark Nights. It was not now such a very difficult problem to guess what the coming Dark Nights might mean. The moon was on the wane: each night there was a longer interval of darkness. And I now understood to some slight degree at least the reason of the fear of the little Upperworld people for the dark. I wondered vaguely what foul villainy it might be that the Morlocks did under the new moon. I felt pretty sure now that my second hypothesis was all wrong. The Upperworld people might once have been the favoured aristocracy, and the Morlocks their mechanical servants; but that had long since passed away. The two species that had resulted from the evolution of man were sliding down towards, or had already arrived at, an altogether new relationship. The Eloi, like the Carlovingian kings,[1] had decayed to a

mere beautiful futility. They still possessed the earth on suffer-
ance: since the Morlocks, subterranean for innumerable generations, had come at last to find the daylit surface intolerable.
And the Morlocks made their garments, I inferred, and main-
tained them in their habitual needs, perhaps through the survival of an old habit of service. They did it as a standing horse
paws with his foot, or as a man enjoys killing animals in sport:
because ancient and departed necessities had impressed it on
the organism. But, clearly, the old order was already in part
reversed. The Nemesis of the delicate ones was creeping on
apace. Ages ago, thousands of generations ago, man had thrust
his brother man out of the ease and the sunshine. And now that
brother was coming back – changed! Already the Eloi had
begun to learn one old lesson anew. They were becoming re-
acquainted with Fear. And suddenly there came into my head
the memory of the meat I had seen in the Underworld. It seemed
odd how it floated into my mind: not stirred up as it were by
the current of my meditations, but coming in almost like a
question from outside. I tried to recall the form of it. I had a
vague sense of something familiar, but I could not tell what it
was at the time.

'Still, however helpless the little people in the presence of
their mysterious Fear, I was differently constituted. I came out
of this age of ours, this ripe prime of the human race, when
Fear does not paralyse and mystery has lost its terrors. I at least
would defend myself. Without further delay I determined to
make myself arms and a fastness where I might sleep. With that
refuge as a base, I could face this strange world with some of
that confidence I had lost in realizing to what creatures night
by night I lay exposed. I felt I could never sleep again until my
bed was secure from them. I shuddered with horror to think
how they must already have examined me.

'I wandered during the afternoon along the valley of the
Thames, but found nothing that commended itself to my mind
as inaccessible. All the buildings and trees seemed easily practi-
cable to such dexterous climbers as the Morlocks, to judge by
their wells, must be. Then the tall pinnacles of the Palace of
Green Porcelain and the polished gleam of its walls came back

to my memory; and in the evening, taking Weena like a child upon my shoulder, I went up the hills towards the south-west. The distance, I had reckoned, was seven or eight miles, but it must have been nearer eighteen. I had first seen the place on a moist afternoon when distances are deceptively diminished. In addition, the heel of one of my shoes was loose, and a nail was working through the sole – they were comfortable old shoes I wore about indoors – so that I was lame. And it was already long past sunset when I came in sight of the palace, silhouetted black against the pale yellow of the sky.

'Weena had been hugely delighted when I began to carry her, but after a time she desired me to let her down, and ran along by the side of me, occasionally darting off on either hand to pick flowers to stick in my pockets. My pockets had always puzzled Weena, but at the last she had concluded that they were an eccentric kind of vase for floral decoration. At least she utilized them for that purpose. And that reminds me! In changing my jacket I found . . .'

The Time Traveller paused, put his hand into his pocket, and silently placed two withered flowers, not unlike very large white mallows, upon the little table. Then he resumed his narrative.

'As the hush of evening crept over the world and we proceeded over the hill crest towards Wimbledon, Weena grew tired and wanted to return to the house of grey stone. But I pointed out the distant pinnacles of the Palace of Green Porcelain to her, and contrived to make her understand that we were seeking a refuge there from her Fear. You know that great pause that comes upon things before the dusk? Even the breeze stops in the trees. To me there is always an air of expectation about that evening stillness. The sky was clear, remote and empty save for a few horizontal bars far down in the sunset. Well, that night the expectation took the colour of my fears. In that darkling calm my senses seemed preternaturally sharpened. I fancied I could even feel the hollowness of the ground beneath my feet: could, indeed, almost see through it the Morlocks in their anthill going hither and thither and waiting for the dark. In my excitement I fancied that they would receive my invasion of their burrows as a declaration of war. And why had they taken my Time Machine?

'So we went on in the quiet, and the twilight deepened into night. The clear blue of the distance faded, and one star after another came out. The ground grew dim and the trees black. Weena's fears and her fatigue grew upon her. I took her in my arms and talked to her and caressed her. Then, as the darkness grew deeper, she put her arms round my neck, and, closing her eyes, tightly pressed her face against my shoulder. So we went down a long slope into a valley, and there in the dimness I almost walked into a little river. This I waded, and went up the opposite side of the valley, past a number of sleeping houses, and by a statue – a Faun, or some such figure, *minus* the head. Here too were acacias. So far I had seen nothing of the Morlocks, but it was yet early in the night, and the darker hours before the old moon rose were still to come.

'From the brow of the next hill I saw a thick wood spreading wide and black before me. I hesitated at this. I could see no end to it, either to the right or the left. Feeling tired – my feet in particular, were very sore – I carefully lowered Weena from my shoulder as I halted, and sat down upon the turf. I could no longer see the Palace of Green Porcelain, and I was in doubt of my direction. I looked into the thickness of the wood and thought of what it might hide. Under that dense tangle of branches one would be out of sight of the stars. Even were there no other lurking danger – a danger I did not care to let my imagination loose upon – there would still be all the roots to stumble over and the tree-boles to strike against. I was very tired, too, after the excitements of the day; so I decided that I would not face it, but would pass the night upon the open hill.

'Weena, I was glad to find, was fast asleep. I carefully wrapped her in my jacket, and sat down beside her to wait for the moonrise. The hillside was quiet and deserted, but from the black of the wood there came now and then a stir of living things. Above me shone the stars, for the night was very clear. I felt a certain sense of friendly comfort in their twinkling. All the old constellations had gone from the sky, however: that slow movement which is imperceptible in a hundred human

lifetimes, had long since rearranged them in unfamiliar group-
ings. But the Milky Way, it seemed to me, was still the same
tattered streamer of star-dust as of yore. Southward (as I judged
it) was a very bright red star that was new to me; it was even
more splendid than our own green Sirius.[2] And amid all these
scintillating points of light one bright planet[3] shone kindly and
steadily like the face of an old friend.

'Looking at these stars suddenly dwarfed my own troubles
and all the gravities of terrestrial life. I thought of their unfath-
omable distance, and the slow inevitable drift of their movements out of the unknown past into the unknown future. I
thought of the great precessional cycle that the pole of the earth
describes. Only forty times[4] had that silent revolution occurred
during all the years that I had traversed. And during these
few revolutions all the activity, all the traditions, the complex
organizations, the nations, languages, literatures, aspirations,
even the mere memory of Man as I knew him, had been swept
out of existence. Instead were these frail creatures who had
forgotten their high ancestry, and the white Things of which
I went in terror. Then I thought of the Great Fear that was
between the two species, and for the first time, with a sudden
shiver, came the clear knowledge of what the meat I had seen
might be. Yet it was too horrible! I looked at little Weena
sleeping beside me, her face white and starlike under the stars,
and forthwith dismissed the thought.

'Through that long night I held my mind off the Morlocks as
well as I could, and whiled away the time by trying to fancy I
could find signs of the old constellations in the new confusion.
The sky kept very clear, except for a hazy cloud or so. No
doubt I dozed at times. Then, as my vigil wore on, came a
faintness in the eastward sky, like the reflection of some colourless fire, and the old moon rose, thin and peaked and white.
And close behind, and overtaking it, and overflowing it, the
dawn came, pale at first, and then growing pink and warm. No
Morlocks had approached us. Indeed, I had seen none upon
the hill that night. And in the confidence of renewed day it
almost seemed to me that my fear had been unreasonable. I
stood up and found my foot with the loose heel swollen at the

ankle and painful under the heel; so I sat down again, took off my shoes and flung them away.

'I awakened Weena, and we went down into the wood, now green and pleasant instead of black and forbidding. We found some fruit wherewith to break our fast. We soon met others of the dainty ones, laughing and dancing in the sunlight as though there was no such thing in nature as the night. And then I thought once more of the meat that I had seen. I felt assured now of what it was, and from the bottom of my heart I pitied this last feeble rill from the great flood of humanity. Clearly, at some time in the Long-Ago of human decay the Morlocks' food had run short. Possibly they had lived on rats and suchlike vermin. Even now man is far less discriminating and exclusive in his food than he was – far less than any monkey. His prejudice against human flesh is no deep-seated instinct. And so these inhuman sons of men—! I tried to look at the thing in a scientific spirit. After all, they were less human and more remote than our cannibal ancestors of three or four thousand years ago. And the intelligence that would have made this state of things a torment had gone. Why should I trouble myself? These Eloi were mere fatted cattle, which the ant-like Morlocks preserved and preyed upon – probably saw to the breeding of. And there was Weena dancing at my side!

'Then I tried to preserve myself from the horror that was coming upon me, by regarding it as a rigorous punishment of human selfishness. Man had been content to live in ease and delight upon the labours of his fellow man, had taken Necessity as his watchword and excuse, and in the fulness of time Necessity had come home to him. I even tried a Carlyle-like scorn of this wretched aristocracy in decay.[5] But this attitude of mind was impossible. However great their intellectual degradation, the Eloi had kept too much of the human form not to claim my sympathy, and to make me perforce a sharer in their degradation and their Fear.

'I had at that time very vague ideas as to the course I should pursue. My first was to secure some safe place of refuge, and to make myself such arms of metal or stone as I could contrive. That necessity was immediate. In the next place, I hoped to procure some means of fire, so that I should have the weapon of a torch at hand, for nothing, I knew, would be more efficient against these Morlocks. Then I wanted to arrange some contrivance to break open the doors of bronze under the White Sphinx. I had in mind a battering-ram. I had a persuasion that if I could enter those doors and carry a blaze of light before me I should discover the Time Machine and escape. I could not imagine the Morlocks were strong enough to move it far away. Weena I had resolved to bring with me to our own time. And turning such schemes over in my mind I pursued our way towards the building which my fancy had chosen as our dwelling.

8

'I found the Palace of Green Porcelain, when we approached it about noon, deserted and falling into ruin. Only ragged vestiges of glass remained in its windows, and great sheets of the green facing had fallen away from the corroded metallic framework. It lay very high upon a turfy down, and looking north-eastward before I entered it, I was surprised to see a large estuary, or even creek, where I judged Wandsworth and Battersea must once have been. I thought then – though I never followed up the thought – of what might have happened, or might be happening, to the living things in the sea.

'The material of the Palace proved on examination to be indeed porcelain, and along the face of it I saw an inscription in some unknown character. I thought, rather foolishly, that Weena might help me to interpret this, but I only learnt that the bare idea of writing had never entered her head. She always seemed to me, I fancy, more human than she was, perhaps because her affection was so human.

'Within the big valves of the door – which were open and broken – we found, instead of the customary hall, a long gallery lit by many side windows. At the first glance I was reminded of a museum. The tiled floor was thick with dust, and a remarkable array of miscellaneous objects was shrouded in the same grey covering. Then I perceived, standing strange and gaunt in the centre of the hall, what was clearly the lower part of a huge skeleton. I recognized by the oblique feet that it was some extinct creature after the fashion of the Megatherium.[1] The skull and the upper bones lay beside it in the thick dust, and in one place, where rain-water had dropped through a leak in the

roof, the thing itself had been worn away. Further in the gallery
was the huge skeleton barrel of a Brontosaurus.[2] My museum
hypothesis was confirmed. Going towards the side I found what
appeared to be sloping shelves, and, clearing away the thick
dust, I found the old familiar glass cases of our own time. But
they must have been airtight, to judge from the fair preservation
of some of their contents.

'Clearly we stood among the ruins of some latter-day South
Kensington![3] Here, apparently, was the Palaeontological Section, and a very splendid array of fossils it must have been,
though the inevitable process of decay that had been staved off
for a time, and had, through the extinction of bacteria and
fungi, lost ninety-nine hundredths of its force, was, nevertheless,
with extreme sureness if with extreme slowness at work again
upon all its treasures. Here and there I found traces of the little
people in the shape of rare fossils broken to pieces or threaded
in strings upon reeds. And the cases had in some instances been
bodily removed – by the Morlocks as I judged. The place was
very silent. The thick dust deadened our footsteps. Weena, who
had been rolling a sea-urchin down the sloping glass of a case,
presently came, as I stared about me, and very quietly took my
hand and stood beside me.

'And at first I was so much surprised by this ancient monument of an intellectual age, that I gave no thought to the possibilities it presented. Even my preoccupation about the Time
Machine receded a little from my mind.

'To judge from the size of the place, this Palace of Green
Porcelain had a great deal more in it than a Gallery of Palaeon-
tology; possibly historical galleries; it might be, even a library!
To me, at least in my present circumstances, these would be
vastly more interesting than this spectacle of old-time geology
in decay. Exploring, I found another short gallery running
transversely to the first. This appeared to be devoted to min-
erals, and the sight of a block of sulphur set my mind running
on gunpowder. But I could find no saltpetre; indeed, no nitrates
of any kind. Doubtless they had deliquesced ages ago. Yet the
sulphur hung in my mind, and set up a train of thinking. As for
the rest of the contents of that gallery, though on the whole

they were the best preserved of all I saw, I had little interest. I am no specialist in mineralogy, and I went on down a very ruinous aisle running parallel to the first hall I had entered. Apparently this section had been devoted to natural history, but everything had long since passed out of recognition. A few shrivelled and blackened vestiges of what had once been stuffed animals, desiccated mummies in jars that had once held spirit, a brown dust of departed plants; that was all! I was sorry for that, because I should have been glad to trace the patient readjustments by which the conquest of animated nature had been attained. Then we came to a gallery of simply colossal proportions, but singularly ill-lit, the floor of it running downward at a slight angle from the end at which I entered. At intervals white globes hung from the ceiling – many of them cracked and smashed – which suggested that originally the place had been artificially lit. Here I was more in my element, for rising on either side of me were the huge bulks of big machines, all greatly corroded and many broken down, but some still fairly complete. You know I have a certain weakness for mechanism, and I was inclined to linger among these; the more so as for the most part they had the interest of puzzles, and I could make only the vaguest guesses at what they were for. I fancied that if I could solve their puzzles I should find myself in possession of powers that might be of use against the Morlocks.

'Suddenly Weena came very close to my side. So suddenly that she startled me. Had it not been for her I do not think I should have noticed that the floor of the gallery sloped at all.* The end I had come in at was quite above ground, and was lit by rare slit-like windows. As you went down the length, the ground came up against these windows, until at last there was a pit like the "area" of a London house before each, and only a narrow line of daylight at the top. I went slowly along, puzzling about the machines, and had been too intent upon them to notice the gradual diminution of the light, until Weena's

---

* It may be, of course, that the floor did not slope, but that the museum was built into the side of a hill. – ED.

increasing apprehensions drew my attention. Then I saw that
the gallery ran down at last into a thick darkness. I hesitated,
and then, as I looked round me, I saw that the dust was less
abundant and its surface less even. Further away towards the
dimness, it appeared to be broken by a number of small narrow
footprints. My sense of the immediate presence of the Morlocks
revived at that. I felt that I was wasting my time in this academic
examination of machinery. I called to mind that it was already
far advanced in the afternoon, and that I had still no weapon,
no refuge, and no means of making a fire. And then down in
the remote blackness of the gallery I heard a peculiar pattering,
and the same odd noises I had heard down the well.

'I took Weena's hand. Then, struck with a sudden idea, I left
her and turned to a machine from which projected a lever not
unlike those in a signal-box. Clambering upon the stand, and
grasping this lever in my hands, I put all my weight upon it
sideways. Suddenly Weena, deserted in the central aisle, began
to whimper. I had judged the strength of the lever pretty cor-
rectly, for it snapped after a minute's strain, and I rejoined her
with a mace in my hand more than sufficient, I judged, for any
Morlock skull I might encounter. And I longed very much to
kill a Morlock or so. Very inhuman, you may think, to want
to go killing one's own descendants! But it was impossible,
somehow, to feel any humanity in the things. Only my disincli-
nation to leave Weena, and a persuasion that if I began to slake
my thirst for murder my Time Machine might suffer, restrained
me from going straight down the gallery and killing the brutes
I heard.

'Well, mace in one hand and Weena in the other, I went out
of that gallery and into another and still larger one, which at
the first glance reminded me of a military chapel hung with
tattered flags. The brown and charred rags that hung from the
sides of it, I presently recognized as the decaying vestiges of
books. They had long since dropped to pieces, and every sem-
blance of print had left them. But here and there were warped
boards and cracked metallic clasps that told the tale well
enough. Had I been a literary man I might, perhaps, have
moralized upon the futility of all ambition. But as it was, the

thing that struck me with keenest force was the enormous waste of labour to which this sombre wilderness of rotting paper testified. At the time I will confess that I thought chiefly of the *Philosophical Transactions*[4] and my own seventeen papers upon physical optics.

'Then, going up a broad staircase, we came to what may once have been a gallery of technical chemistry. And here I had not a little hope of useful discoveries. Except at one end where the roof had collapsed, this gallery was well preserved. I went eagerly to every unbroken case. And at last, in one of the really airtight cases, I found a box of matches. Very eagerly I tried them. They were perfectly good. They were not even damp. I turned to Weena. "Dance," I cried to her in her own tongue. For now I had a weapon indeed against the horrible creatures we feared. And so, in that derelict museum, upon the thick soft carpeting of dust, to Weena's huge delight, I solemnly performed a kind of composite dance, whistling *The Land of the Leal*[5] as cheerfully as I could. In part it was a modest *cancan*, in part a step-dance, in part a skirt-dance (so far as my tail-coat permitted) and in part original. For I am naturally inventive, as you know.

'Now, I still think that for this box of matches to have escaped the wear of time for immemorial years was most strange, as for me it was a most fortunate thing. Yet, oddly enough, I found a far unlikelier substance, and that was camphor. I found it in a sealed jar, that by chance, I suppose, had been really hermetically sealed. I fancied at first that it was paraffin wax, and smashed the glass accordingly. But the odour of camphor was unmistakable. In the universal decay this volatile substance had chanced to survive, perhaps through many thousands of centuries. It reminded me of a sepia painting I had once seen done from the ink of a fossil Belemnite[6] that must have perished and become fossilized millions of years ago. I was about to throw it away, but I remembered that it was inflammable and burnt with a good bright flame – was, in fact, an excellent candle – and I put it in my pocket. I found no explosives, however, nor any means of breaking down the bronze doors. As yet my iron crowbar was the most helpful thing I had chanced upon. Nevertheless I left that gallery greatly elated.

'I cannot tell you all the story of that long afternoon. It would require a great effort of memory to recall my explorations in at all the proper order. I remember a long gallery of rusting stands of arms, and how I hesitated between my crowbar and a hatchet or a sword. I could not carry both, however, and my bar of iron promised best against the bronze gates. There were numbers of guns, pistols and rifles. The most were masses of rust, but many were of some new metal, and still fairly sound. But any cartridges or powder there may once have been had rotted into dust. One corner I saw was charred and shattered; perhaps, I thought, by an explosion among the specimens. In another place was a vast array of idols – Polynesian, Mexican, Grecian, Phoenician, every country on earth I should think. And here, yielding to an irresistible impulse, I wrote my name upon the nose of a steatite monster from South America that particularly took my fancy.

'As the evening drew on, my interest waned. I went through gallery after gallery, dusty, silent, often ruinous, the exhibits sometimes mere heaps of rust and lignite, sometimes fresher. In one place I suddenly found myself near the model of a tin-mine, and then by the merest accident I discovered, in an airtight case, two dynamite cartridges! I shouted "Eureka," and smashed the case with joy. Then came a doubt. I hesitated. Then, selecting a little side gallery, I made my essay. I never felt such a disappointment as I did in waiting five, ten, fifteen minutes for an explosion that never came. Of course the things were dummies, as I might have guessed from their presence. I really believe that, had they not been so, I should have rushed off incontinently and blown sphinx, bronze doors and (as it proved) my chances of finding the Time Machine, all together into non-existence.

'It was after that, I think, that we came to a little open court within the palace. It was turfed, and had three fruit-trees. So we rested and refreshed ourselves. Towards sunset I began to consider our position. Night was creeping upon us, and my inaccessible hiding-place had still to be found. But that troubled me very little now. I had in my possession a thing that was, perhaps, the best of all defences against the Morlocks – I had

matches! I had the camphor in my pocket, too, if a blaze were
needed. It seemed to me that the best thing we could do would
be to pass the night in the open, protected by a fire. In the
morning there was the getting of the Time Machine. Towards
that, as yet, I had only my iron mace. But now, with my growing
knowledge, I felt very differently towards those bronze doors.
Up to this, I had refrained from forcing them, largely because
of the mystery on the other side. They had never impressed me
as being very strong, and I hoped to find my bar of iron not
altogether inadequate for the work.

9

'We emerged from the palace while the sun was still in part above the horizon. I was determined to reach the White Sphinx early the next morning, and ere the dusk I purposed pushing through the woods that had stopped me on the previous journey. My plan was to go as far as possible that night, and then, building a fire, to sleep in the protection of its glare. Accordingly, as we went along I gathered any sticks or dried grass I saw, and presently had my arms full of such litter. Thus loaded, our progress was slower than I had anticipated, and besides Weena was tired. And I began to suffer from sleepiness too; so that it was full night before we reached the wood. Upon the shrubby hill of its edge Weena would have stopped, fearing the darkness before us; but a singular sense of impending calamity, that should indeed have served me as a warning, drove me onward. I had been without sleep for a night and two days, and I was feverish and irritable. I felt sleep coming upon me, and the Morlocks with it.

'While we hesitated, among the black bushes behind us, and dim against their blackness, I saw three crouching figures. There was scrub and long grass all about us, and I did not feel safe from their insidious approach. The forest, I calculated, was rather less than a mile across. If we could get through it to the bare hillside, there, as it seemed to me, was an altogether safer resting-place; I thought that with my matches and my camphor I could contrive to keep my path illuminated through the woods. Yet it was evident that if I was to flourish matches with my hands I should have to abandon my firewood; so, rather reluctantly, I put it down. And then it came into my head that I would amaze our friends behind by lighting it. I was to discover the atrocious folly of this proceeding, but it came to my mind as an ingenious move for covering our retreat.

'I don't know if you have ever thought what a rare thing flame must be in the absence of man and in a temperate climate. The sun's heat is rarely strong enough to burn, even when it is focused by dewdrops, as is sometimes the case in more tropical districts. Lightning may blast and blacken, but it rarely gives rise to widespread fire. Decaying vegetation may occasionally smoulder with the heat of its fermentation, but this rarely results in flame. In this decadence, too, the art of fire-making had been forgotten on the earth. The red tongues that went licking up my heap of wood were an altogether new and strange thing to Weena.

'She wanted to run to it and play with it. I believe she would have cast herself into it had I not restrained her. But I caught her up, and, in spite of her struggles, plunged boldly before me into the wood. For a little way the glare of my fire lit the path. Looking back presently, I could see, through the crowded stems, that from my heap of sticks the blaze had spread to some bushes adjacent, and a curved line of fire was creeping up the grass of the hill. I laughed at that, and turned again to the dark trees before me. It was very black, and Weena clung to me convulsively, but there was still, as my eyes grew accustomed to the darkness, sufficient light for me to avoid the stems. Overhead it was simply black, except where a gap of remote blue sky shone down upon us here and there. I struck none of my matches because I had no hand free. Upon my left arm I carried my little one, in my right hand I had my iron bar.

'For some way I heard nothing but the crackling twigs under my feet, the faint rustle of the breeze above, and my own breathing and the throb of the blood vessels in my ears. Then I seemed to know of a pattering about me. I pushed on grimly. The pattering grew more distinct, and then I caught the same queer sounds and voices I had heard in the Underworld. There were evidently several of the Morlocks, and they were closing in upon me. Indeed, in another minute I felt a tug at my coat, then something at my arm. And Weena shivered violently, and became quite still.

'It was time for a match. But to get one I must put her down. I did so, and, as I fumbled with my pocket, a struggle began in the darkness about my knees, perfectly silent on her part and with the same peculiar cooing sounds from the Morlocks. Soft little hands, too, were creeping over my coat and back, touching even my neck. Then the match scratched and fizzed. I held it flaring, and saw the white backs of the Morlocks in flight amid the trees. I hastily took a lump of camphor from my pocket, and prepared to light it as soon as the match should wane. Then I looked at Weena. She was lying clutching my feet and quite motionless, with her face to the ground. With a sudden fright I stooped to her. She seemed scarcely to breathe. I lit the block of camphor and flung it to the ground, and as it spat and flared up and drove back the Morlocks and the shadows, I knelt down and lifted her. The wood behind seemed full of the stir and murmur of a great company!

'She seemed to have fainted. I put her carefully upon my shoulder and rose to push on, and then there came a horrible realization. In manoeuvring with my matches and Weena, I had turned myself about several times, and now I had not the faintest idea in what direction lay my path. For all I knew, I might be facing back towards the Palace of Green Porcelain. I found myself in a cold sweat. I had to think rapidly what to do. I determined to build a fire and encamp where we were. I put Weena, still motionless, down upon a turfy bole, and very hastily, as my first lump of camphor waned, I began collecting sticks and leaves. Here and there out of the darkness round me the Morlocks' eyes shone like carbuncles.[1]

'The camphor flickered and went out. I lit a match, and as I did so, two white forms that had been approaching Weena dashed hastily away. One was so blinded by the light that he came straight for me and I felt his bones grind under the blow of my fist. He gave a whoop of dismay, staggered a little way, and fell down. I lit another piece of camphor, and went on gathering my bonfire. Presently I noticed how dry was some of the foliage above me, for since my arrival on the Time Machine, a matter of a week, no rain had fallen. So, instead of casting about among the trees for fallen twigs, I began leaping up and dragging down branches. Very soon I had a choking smoky fire of green wood and dry sticks, and could economize my camphor. Then I turned to where Weena lay beside my iron mace. I tried what I could to revive her, but she lay like one dead. I could not even satisfy myself whether or not she breathed.

'Now, the smoke of the fire beat over towards me, and it must have made me heavy of a sudden. Moreover, the vapour of camphor was in the air. My fire would not need replenishing for an hour or so. I felt very weary after my exertion, and sat down. The wood, too, was full of a slumbrous murmur that I did not understand. I seemed just to nod and open my eyes. But all was dark, and the Morlocks had their hands upon me. Flinging off their clinging fingers I hastily felt in my pocket for the matchbox, and – it had gone! Then they gripped and closed with me again. In a moment I knew what had happened. I had slept, and my fire had gone out, and the bitterness of death came over my soul. The forest seemed full of the smell of burning wood. I was caught by the neck, by the hair, by the arms, and pulled down. It was indescribably horrible in the darkness to feel all these soft creatures heaped upon me. I felt as if I was in a monstrous spider's web. I was overpowered, and went down. I felt little teeth nipping at my neck. I rolled over, and as I did so my hand came against my iron lever. It gave me strength. I struggled up, shaking the human rats from me, and, holding the bar short, I thrust where I judged their faces might be. I could feel the succulent giving of flesh and bone under my blows, and for a moment I was free.

'The strange exultation that so often seems to accompany hard fighting came upon me. I knew that both I and Weena were lost, but I determined to make the Morlocks pay for their meat. I stood with my back to a tree, swinging the iron bar before me. The whole wood was full of the stir and cries of them. A minute passed. Their voices seemed to rise to a higher pitch of excitement, and their movements grew faster. Yet none came within reach. I stood glaring at the blackness. Then suddenly came hope. What if the Morlocks were afraid? And close on the heels of that came a strange thing. The darkness seemed to grow luminous. Very dimly I began to see the Morlocks about me – three battered at my feet – and then I recognized, with incredulous surprise, that the others were running, in an incessant stream, as it seemed, from behind me, and away through the wood in front. And their backs seemed no longer white, but reddish. As I stood agape, I saw a little red spark go drifting across a gap of starlight between the branches, and vanish. And at that I understood the smell of burning wood, the slumbrous murmur that was growing now into a gusty roar, the red glow and the Morlocks' flight.

'Stepping out from behind my tree and looking back, I saw, through the black pillars of the nearer trees, the flames of the burning forest. It was my first fire coming after me. With that I looked for Weena, but she was gone. The hissing and crackling behind me, the explosive thud as each fresh tree burst into flame, left little time for reflection. My iron bar still gripped, I followed in the Morlocks' path. It was a close race. Once the flames crept forward so swiftly on my right as I ran that I was outflanked and had to strike off to the left. But at last I emerged upon a small open space, and as I did so, a Morlock came blundering towards me, and past me, and went on straight into the fire!

'And now I was to see the most weird and horrible thing, I think, of all that I beheld in that future age. This whole space was as bright as day with the reflection of the fire. In the centre was a hillock or tumulus, surmounted by a scorched hawthorn. Beyond this was another arm of the burning forest, with yellow tongues already writhing from it, completely encircling the space with a fence of fire. Upon the hillside were some thirty or forty Morlocks, dazzled by the light and heat, and blundering hither and thither against each other in their bewilderment. At first I did not realize their blindness, and struck furiously at them with my bar, in a frenzy of fear, as they approached me, killing one and crippling several more. But when I had watched the gestures of one of them groping under the hawthorn against the red sky, and heard their moans, I was assured of their

absolute helplessness and misery in the glare, and I struck no
more of them.

'Yet every now and then one would come straight towards
me, setting loose a quivering horror that made me quick to
elude him. At one time the flames died down somewhat, and I
feared the foul creatures would presently be able to see me. I
was even thinking of beginning the fight by killing some of them
before this should happen; but the fire burst out again brightly,
and I stayed my hand. I walked about the hill among them and
avoided them, looking for some trace of Weena. But Weena
was gone.

'At last I sat down on the summit of the hillock, and watched
this strange incredible company of blind things groping to and
fro, and making uncanny noises to each other, as the glare of
the fire beat on them. The coiling uprush of smoke streamed
across the sky, and through the rare tatters of that red canopy,
remote as though they belonged to another universe, shone
the little stars. Two or three Morlocks came blundering into
me, and I drove them off with blows of my fists, trembling as
I did so.

'For the most part of that night I was persuaded it was a
nightmare. I bit myself and screamed in a passionate desire to
awake. I beat the ground with my hands, and got up and sat
down again, and wandered here and there, and again sat down.
Then I would fall to rubbing my eyes and calling upon God to
let me awake. Thrice I saw Morlocks put their heads down in
a kind of agony and rush into the flames. But, at last, above the
subsiding red of the fire, above the streaming masses of black
smoke and the whitening and blackening tree stumps, and the
diminishing numbers of these dim creatures, came the white
light of the day.

'I searched again for traces of Weena, but there were none.
It was plain that they had left her poor little body in the forest.
I cannot describe how it relieved me to think that it had escaped
the awful fate to which it seemed destined. As I thought of
that, I was almost moved to begin a massacre of the helpless
abominations about me, but I contained myself. The hillock, as
I have said, was a kind of island in the forest. From its summit

I could now make out through a haze of smoke the Palace of Green Porcelain, and from that I could get my bearings for the White Sphinx. And so, leaving the remnant of these damned souls still going hither and thither and moaning, as the day grew clearer, I tied some grass about my feet and limped on across smoking ashes and among black stems, that still pulsated internally with fire, towards the hiding-place of the Time Machine. I walked slowly, for I was almost exhausted, as well as lame, and I felt the intensest wretchedness for the horrible death of little Weena. It seemed an overwhelming calamity. Now, in this old familiar room, it is more like the sorrow of a dream than an actual loss. But that morning it left me absolutely lonely again – terribly alone. I began to think of this house of mine, of this fireside, of some of you, and with such thoughts came a longing that was pain.

'But, as I walked over the smoking ashes under the bright morning sky, I made a discovery. In my trouser pocket were still some loose matches. The box must have leaked before it was lost.

10

'About eight or nine in the morning I came to the same seat of yellow metal from which I had viewed the world upon the evening of my arrival. I thought of my hasty conclusions upon that evening and could not refrain from laughing bitterly at my confidence. Here was the same beautiful scene, the same abundant foliage, the same splendid palaces and magnificent ruins, the same silver river running between its fertile banks. The gay robes of the beautiful people moved hither and thither among the trees. Some were bathing in exactly the place where I had saved Weena, and that suddenly gave me a keen stab of pain. And like blots upon the landscape rose the cupolas above the ways to the Underworld. I understood now what all the beauty of the Upperworld people covered. Very pleasant was their day, as pleasant as the day of the cattle in the field. Like the cattle, they knew of no enemies and provided against no needs. And their end was the same.

'I grieved to think how brief the dream of the human intellect had been. It had committed suicide. It had set itself steadfastly towards comfort and ease, a balanced society with security and permanency as its watchword, it had attained its hopes – to come to this at last. Once, life and property must have reached almost absolute safety. The rich had been assured of his wealth and comfort, the toiler assured of his life and work. No doubt in that perfect world there had been no unemployed problem, no social question left unsolved. And a great quiet had followed.

'It is a law of nature we overlook, that intellectual versatility is the compensation for change, danger and trouble. An animal perfectly in harmony with its environment is a perfect mechanism. Nature never appeals to intelligence until habit and instinct are useless. There is no intelligence where there is no change and no need of change. Only those animals partake of intelligence that have to meet a huge variety of needs and dangers.[1]

'So, as I see it, the Upperworld man had drifted towards his feeble prettiness, and the Underworld to mere mechanical industry. But that perfect state had lacked one thing even for mechanical perfection – absolute permanency. Apparently as time went on, the feeding of the Underworld, however it was effected, had become disjointed. Mother Necessity, who had been staved off for a few thousand years, came back again, and she began below. The Underworld being in contact with machinery, which, however perfect, still needs some little thought outside habit, had probably retained perforce rather more initiative, if less of every other human character, than the upper. And when other meat failed them, they turned to what old habit had hitherto forbidden. So I say I saw it in my last view of the world of Eight Hundred and Two Thousand Seven Hundred and One. It may be as wrong an explanation as mortal wit could invent. It is how the thing shaped itself to me, and as that I give it to you.

'After the fatigues, excitements, and terrors of the past days, and in spite of my grief, this seat and the tranquil view and the warm sunlight were very pleasant. I was very tired and sleepy, and soon my theorizing passed into dozing. Catching myself at that, I took my own hint, and spreading myself out upon the turf I had a long and refreshing sleep.

'I awoke a little before sunsetting. I now felt safe against being caught napping by the Morlocks, and, stretching myself, I came on down the hill towards the White Sphinx. I had my crowbar in one hand, and the other hand played with the matches in my pocket.

'And now came a most unexpected thing. As I approached the pedestal of the sphinx I found the bronze valves were open. They had slid down into grooves.

'At that I stopped short before them, hesitating to enter.

'Within was a small apartment, and on a raised place in the corner of this was the Time Machine. I had the small levers in my pocket. So here, after all my elaborate preparations for the siege of the White Sphinx, was a meek surrender. I threw my iron bar away, almost sorry not to use it.

'A sudden thought came into my head as I stooped towards the portal. For once, at least, I grasped the mental operations of the Morlocks. Suppressing a strong inclination to laugh, I stepped through the bronze frame and up to the Time Machine. I was surprised to find it had been carefully oiled and cleaned. I have suspected since that the Morlocks had even partially taken it to pieces while trying in their dim way to grasp its purpose.

'Now as I stood and examined it, finding a pleasure in the mere touch of the contrivance, the thing I had expected happened. The bronze panels suddenly slid up and struck the frame with a clang. I was in the dark – trapped. So the Morlocks thought. At that I chuckled gleefully.

'I could already hear their murmuring laughter as they came towards me. Very calmly I tried to strike the match. I had only to fix on the levers and depart then like a ghost. But I had overlooked one little thing. The matches were of that abominable kind that light only on the box.

'You may imagine how all my calm vanished. The little brutes were close upon me. One touched me. I made a sweeping blow in the dark at them with the levers, and began to scramble into the saddle of the machine. Then came one hand upon me and then another. Then I had simply to fight against their persistent fingers for my levers, and at the same time feel for the studs over which these fitted. One, indeed, they almost got away from me. As it slipped from my hand, I had to butt in the dark with my head – I could hear the Morlock's skull ring – to recover it. It was a nearer thing than the fight in the forest, I think, this last scramble.

'But at last the lever was fixed and pulled over. The clinging hands slipped from me. The darkness presently fell from my eyes. I found myself in the same grey light and tumult I have already described.

11

'I have already told you of the sickness and confusion that comes with time travelling. And this time I was not seated properly in the saddle, but sideways and in an unstable fashion. For an indefinite time I clung to the machine as it swayed and vibrated, quite unheeding how I went, and when I brought myself to look at the dials again I was amazed to find where I had arrived. One dial records days, another thousands of days, another millions of days, and another thousands of millions. Now, instead of reversing the levers I had pulled them over so as to go forward with them, and when I came to look at these indicators I found that the thousands hand was sweeping round as fast as the seconds hand of a watch – into futurity.

'As I drove on, a peculiar change crept over the appearance of things. The palpitating greyness grew darker; then – though I was still travelling with prodigious velocity – the blinking succession of day and night, which was usually indicative of a slower pace, returned, and grew more and more marked. This puzzled me very much at first. The alternations of night and day grew slower and slower, and so did the passage of the sun across the sky, until they seemed to stretch through centuries. At last a steady twilight brooded over the earth, a twilight only broken now and then when a comet glared across the darkling sky. The band of light that had indicated the sun had long since disappeared; for the sun had ceased to set – it simply rose and fell in the west, and grew ever broader and more red. All trace of the moon had vanished. The circling of the stars, growing slower and slower, had given place to creeping points of light. At last, some time before I stopped, the sun, red and very large, halted motionless upon the horizon, a vast dome glowing with a dull heat, and now and then suffering a momentary extinction. At one time it had for a little while glowed more brilliantly again, but it speedily reverted to its sullen red heat. I perceived by this slowing down of its rising and setting that the work of the tidal drag was done.[1] The earth had come to rest with one face to the sun, even as in our own time the moon faces the earth. Very cautiously, for I remembered my former headlong fall, I began to reverse my motion. Slower and slower went the circling hands until the thousands one seemed motionless and the daily one was no longer a mere mist upon its scale. Still slower, until the dim outlines of a desolate beach grew visible.

'I stopped very gently and sat upon the Time Machine, looking round. The sky was no longer blue. North-eastward it was inky black, and out of the blackness shone brightly and steadily the pale white stars. Overhead it was a deep Indian red and starless, and south-eastward it grew brighter to a glowing scarlet where, cut by the horizon, lay the huge hull of the sun, red and motionless. The rocks about me were of a harsh reddish colour, and all the trace of life that I could see at first was the intensely green vegetation that covered every projecting point on their south-eastern face. It was the same rich green that one sees on forest moss or on the lichen in caves: plants which like these grow in a perpetual twilight.

'The machine was standing on a sloping beach. The sea stretched away to the south-west, to rise into a sharp bright horizon against the wan sky. There were no breakers and no waves, for not a breath of wind was stirring. Only a slight oily swell rose and fell like a gentle breathing, and showed that the eternal sea was still moving and living. And along the margin where the water sometimes broke was a thick incrustation of salt – pink under the lurid sky. There was a sense of oppression in my head, and I noticed that I was breathing very fast. The sensation reminded me of my only experience of mountaineering, and from that I judged the air to be more rarefied than it is now.

'Far away up the desolate slope I heard a harsh scream, and saw a thing like a huge white butterfly go slanting and fluttering up into the sky and, circling, disappear over some low hillocks beyond. The sound of its voice was so dismal that I shivered and seated myself more firmly upon the machine. Looking round me again, I saw that, quite near, what I had taken to be a reddish mass of rock was moving slowly towards me. Then I saw the thing was really a monstrous crab-like creature. Can you imagine a crab as large as yonder table, with its many legs moving slowly and uncertainly, its big claws swaying, its long antennae, like carters' whips, waving and feeling, and its stalked eyes gleaming at you on either side of its metallic front? Its back was corrugated and ornamented with ungainly bosses, and a greenish incrustation blotched it here and there. I could see the many palps of its complicated mouth flickering and feeling as it moved.

'As I stared at this sinister apparition crawling towards me, I felt a tickling on my cheek as though a fly had lighted there. I tried to brush it away with my hand, but in a moment it returned, and almost immediately came another by my ear. I struck at this, and caught something threadlike. It was drawn swiftly out of my hand. With a frightful qualm, I turned, and saw that I had grasped the antenna of another monster crab that stood just behind me. Its evil eyes were wriggling on their stalks, its mouth was all alive with appetite, and its vast ungainly claws, smeared with an algal slime, were descending upon me. In a moment my hand was on the lever, and I had placed a month between myself and these monsters. But I was still on the same beach, and I saw them distinctly now as soon as I stopped. Dozens of them seemed to be crawling here and there, in the sombre light, among the foliated sheets of intense green.

'I cannot convey the sense of abominable desolation that hung over the world. The red eastern sky, the northward blackness, the salt Dead Sea,[2] the stony beach crawling with these foul, slow-stirring monsters, the uniform poisonous-looking green of the lichenous plants, the thin air that hurts one's lungs; all contributed to an appalling effect. I moved on a hundred years, and there was the same red sun – a little larger, a little duller – the same dying sea, the same chill air, and the same crowd of earthy crustacea creeping in and out among the green weed and the red rocks. And in the westward sky I saw a curved pale line like a vast new moon.

'So I travelled, stopping ever and again, in great strides of a thousand years or more, drawn on by the mystery of the earth's fate, watching with a strange fascination the sun grow larger and duller in the westward sky, and the life of the old earth ebb away. At last, more than thirty million years hence, the huge red-hot dome of the sun had come to obscure nearly a tenth part of the darkling heavens. Then I stopped once more, for the crawling multitude of crabs had disappeared, and the red beach, save for its livid green liverworts and lichens, seemed lifeless. And now it was flecked with white. A bitter cold assailed me. Rare white flakes ever and again came eddying down. To the north-eastward, the glare of snow lay under the starlight of the sable sky, and I could see an undulating crest of hillocks pinkish white. There were fringes of ice along the sea margin, with drifting masses further out; but the main expanse of that salt ocean, all bloody under the eternal sunset, was still unfrozen.

'I looked about me to see if any traces of animal life remained. A certain indefinable apprehension still kept me in the saddle of the machine. But I saw nothing moving, in earth or sky or sea. The green slime on the rocks alone testified that life was not extinct. A shallow sandbank had appeared in the sea and the water had receded from the beach. I fancied I saw some black object flopping about upon this bank, but it became motionless as I looked at it, and I judged that my eye had been deceived, and that the black object was merely a rock. The stars in the sky were intensely bright and seemed to me to twinkle very little.

'Suddenly I noticed that the circular westward outline of the sun had changed; that a concavity, a bay, had appeared in the curve. I saw this grow larger. For a minute perhaps I stared aghast at this blackness that was creeping over the day, and then I realized that an eclipse was beginning. Either the moon or the planet Mercury was passing across the sun's disk. Naturally, at first I took it to be the moon, but there is much to incline me to believe that what I really saw was the transit of an inner planet passing very near to the earth.

'The darkness grew apace; a cold wind began to blow in freshening gusts from the east, and the showering white flakes in the air increased in number. From the edge of the sea came a ripple and whisper. Beyond these lifeless sounds the world was silent. Silent? It would be hard to convey the stillness of it. All the sounds of man, the bleating of sheep, the cries of birds, the hum of insects, the stir that makes the background of our lives – all that was over. As the darkness thickened, the eddying flakes grew more abundant, dancing before my eyes; and the cold of the air more intense. At last, one by one, swiftly, one after the other, the white peaks of the distant hills vanished into blackness. The breeze rose to a moaning wind. I saw the black central shadow of the eclipse sweeping towards me. In another moment the pale stars alone were visible. All else was rayless obscurity. The sky was absolutely black.

'A horror of this great darkness came on me. The cold, that smote to my marrow, and the pain I felt in breathing, overcame me. I shivered, and a deadly nausea seized me. Then like a red-hot bow in the sky appeared the edge of the sun. I got off the machine to recover myself. I felt giddy and incapable of facing the return journey. As I stood sick and confused I saw again the moving thing upon the shoal – there was no mistake now that it was a moving thing – against the red water of the sea. It was a round thing, the size of a football perhaps, or, it may be, bigger, and tentacles trailed down from it; it seemed black against the weltering blood-red water, and it was hopping fitfully about. Then I felt I was fainting. But a terrible dread of lying helpless in that remote and awful twilight sustained me while I clambered upon the saddle.

'So I came back. For a long time I must have been insensible upon the machine. The blinking succession of the days and nights was resumed, the sun got golden again, the sky blue. I breathed with greater freedom. The fluctuating contours of the land ebbed and flowed. The hands spun backward upon the dials. At last I saw again the dim shadows of houses, the evidences of decadent humanity. These, too, changed and passed, and others came. Presently, when the million dial was at zero, I slackened speed. I began to recognize our own petty and familiar architecture, the thousands hand ran back to the starting-point, the night and day flapped slower and slower. Then the old walls of the laboratory came round me. Very gently, now, I slowed the mechanism down.

'I saw one little thing that seemed odd to me. I think I have told you that when I set out, before my velocity became very high, Mrs Watchett had walked across the room, travelling, as it seemed to me, like a rocket. As I returned, I passed again across that minute when she traversed the laboratory. But now her every motion appeared to be the exact inversion of her previous ones. The door at the lower end opened, and she glided quietly up the laboratory, back foremost, and disappeared behind the door by which she had previously entered. Just before that I seemed to see Hillyer[1] for a moment; but he passed like a flash.

'Then I stopped the machine, and saw about me again the old familiar laboratory, my tools, my appliances just as I had left them. I got off the thing very shakily, and sat down upon my bench. For several minutes I trembled violently. Then I became calmer. Around me was my old workshop again, exactly as it had been. I might have slept there, and the whole thing have been a dream.

'And yet, not exactly! The thing had started from the south-east corner of the laboratory. It had come to rest again in the north-west, against the wall where you saw it. That gives you the exact distance from my little lawn to the pedestal of the White Sphinx, into which the Morlocks had carried my machine.

'For a time my brain went stagnant. Presently I got up and came through the passage here, limping, because my heel was still painful, and feeling sorely begrimed. I saw the *Pall Mall Gazette*[2] on the table by the door. I found the date was indeed today, and looking at the timepiece, saw the hour was almost eight o'clock. I heard your voices and the clatter of plates. I hesitated – I felt so sick and weak. Then I sniffed good whole-some meat, and opened the door on you. You know the rest. I washed, and dined, and now I am telling you the story.'

'I know,' he said, after a pause, 'that all this will be absolutely incredible to you. To me the one incredible thing is that I am here tonight in this old familiar room, looking into your friendly faces and telling you these strange adventures.'

He looked at the Medical Man. 'No. I cannot expect you to believe it. Take it as a lie – or a prophecy. Say I dreamed it in the workshop. Consider I have been speculating upon the destinies of our race until I have hatched this fiction. Treat my assertion of its truth as a mere stroke of art to enhance its interest. And taking it as a story, what do you think of it?'

He took up his pipe, and began, in his old accustomed manner, to tap with it nervously upon the bars of the grate. There was a momentary stillness. Then chairs began to creak and shoes to scrape upon the carpet. I took my eyes off the Time Traveller's face, and looked round at his audience. They were in the dark, and little spots of colour swam before them. The Medical Man seemed absorbed in the contemplation of our host. The Editor was looking hard at the end of his cigar – the sixth. The Journalist fumbled for his watch. The others, as far as I remember, were motionless.

The Editor stood up with a sigh. 'What a pity it is you're not a writer of stories!' he said, putting his hand on the Time Traveller's shoulder.

'You don't believe it?'

'Well —'

'I thought not.'

The Time Traveller turned to us. 'Where are the matches?' he said. He lit one and spoke over his pipe, puffing. 'To tell you the truth . . . I hardly believe it myself. . . . And yet . . .'

His eye fell with a mute inquiry upon the withered white flowers upon the little table. Then he turned over the hand holding his pipe, and I saw he was looking at some half-healed scars on his knuckles.

The Medical Man rose, came to the lamp, and examined the flowers. 'The gynaeceum's odd,' he said. The Psychologist leant forward to see, holding out his hand for a specimen.

'I'm hanged if it isn't a quarter to one,' said the Journalist. 'How shall we get home?'

'Plenty of cabs at the station,' said the Psychologist.

'It's a curious thing,' said the Medical Man; 'but I certainly don't know the natural order of these flowers. May I have them?'

The Time Traveller hesitated. Then suddenly: 'Certainly not.'

'Where did you really get them?' said the Medical Man.

The Time Traveller put his hand to his head. He spoke like one who was trying to keep hold of an idea that eluded him. 'They were put into my pocket by Weena, when I travelled into Time.' He stared round the room. 'I'm damned if it isn't all going. This room and you and the atmosphere of everyday is too much for my memory. Did I ever make a Time Machine, or a model of a Time Machine? Or is it all only a dream? They say life is a dream, a precious poor dream at times – but I can't stand another that won't fit. It's madness. And where did the dream come from? . . . I must look at that machine. If there *is* one!'

He caught up the lamp swiftly, and carried it, flaring red, through the door into the corridor. We followed him. There in the flickering light of the lamp was the machine sure enough, squat, ugly and askew; a thing of brass, ebony, ivory and translucent glimmering quartz. Solid to the touch – for I put out my hand and felt the rail of it – and with brown spots and smears upon the ivory, and bits of grass and moss upon the lower parts, and one rail bent awry.

The Time Traveller put the lamp down on the bench, and ran his hand along the damaged rail. 'It's all right now,' he said. 'The story I told you was true. I'm sorry to have brought you out here in the cold.' He took up the lamp, and, in an absolute silence, we returned to the smoking-room.

He came into the hall with us and helped the Editor on with his coat. The Medical Man looked into his face and, with a certain hesitation, told him he was suffering from overwork,[3] at which he laughed hugely. I remember him standing in the open doorway, bawling good night.

I shared a cab with the Editor. He thought the tale a 'gaudy lie'. For my own part I was unable to come to a conclusion. The story was so fantastic and incredible, the telling so credible and sober. I lay awake most of the night thinking about it. I determined to go next day and see the Time Traveller again. I was told he was in the laboratory, and being on easy terms in the house, I went up to him. The laboratory, however, was empty. I stared for a minute at the Time Machine and put out my hand and touched the lever. At that the squat substantial-looking mass swayed like a bough shaken by the wind. Its instability startled me extremely, and I had a queer reminiscence of the childish days when I used to be forbidden to meddle. I came back through the corridor. The Time Traveller met me in the smoking-room. He was coming from the house. He had a small camera under one arm and a knapsack under the other. He laughed when he saw me, and gave me an elbow to shake. 'I'm frightfully busy,' said he, 'with that thing in there.'

'But is it not some hoax?' I said. 'Do you really travel through time?'

'Really and truly I do.' And he looked frankly into my eyes. He hesitated. His eye wandered about the room. 'I only want half an hour,' he said. 'I know why you came, and it's awfully good of you. There's some magazines here. If you'll stop to lunch I'll prove you this time travelling up to the hilt, specimens and all. If you'll forgive my leaving you now?'

I consented, hardly comprehending then the full import of his words, and he nodded and went on down the corridor. I heard the door of the laboratory slam, seated myself in a chair and took up a daily paper. What was he going to do before lunchtime? Then suddenly I was reminded by an advertisement that I had promised to meet Richardson, the publisher, at two. I looked at my watch, and saw that I could barely save that engagement. I got up and went down the passage to tell the Time Traveller.

As I took hold of the handle of the door I heard an exclamation, oddly truncated at the end, and a click and a thud. A gust of air whirled round me as I opened the door, and from within came the sound of broken glass falling on the floor. The Time Traveller was not there. I seemed to see a ghostly, indistinct figure sitting in a whirling mass of black and brass for a moment – a figure so transparent that the bench behind with its sheets of drawings was absolutely distinct; but this phantasm vanished as I rubbed my eyes. The Time Machine had gone. Save for a subsiding stir of dust, the further end of the laboratory was empty. A pane of the skylight had, apparently, just been blown in.

I felt an unreasonable amazement. I knew that something strange had happened, and for the moment could not distinguish what the strange thing might be. As I stood staring, the door into the garden opened, and the man-servant appeared.

We looked at each other. Then ideas began to come. 'Has Mr — gone out that way?' said I.

'No, sir. No one has come out this way. I was expecting to find him here.'

At that I understood. At the risk of disappointing Richardson I stayed on, waiting for the Time Traveller; waiting for the second, perhaps still stranger story, and the specimens and photographs he would bring with him. But I am beginning now to fear that I must wait a lifetime. The Time Traveller vanished three years ago. And, as everybody knows now, he has never returned.

Epilogue

One cannot choose but wonder. Will he ever return? It may be that he swept back into the past, and fell among the blood-drinking, hairy savages of the Age of Unpolished Stone; into the abysses of the Cretaceous Sea; or among the grotesque saurians, the huge reptilian brutes of the Jurassic times. He may even now – if I may use the phrase – be wandering on some plesiosaurus[1]-haunted Oolitic[2] coral reef, or beside the lonely saline lakes of the Triassic Age. Or did he go forward, into one of the nearer ages, in which men are still men, but with the riddles of our own time answered and its wearisome problems solved? Into the manhood of the race: for I, for my own part, cannot think that these latter days of weak experiment, fragmentary theory and mutual discord are indeed man's culminating time! I say, for my own part. He, I know – for the question had been discussed among us long before the Time Machine was made – thought but cheerlessly of the Advancement of Mankind, and saw in the growing pile of civilization only a foolish heaping that must inevitably fall back upon and destroy its makers in the end. If that is so, it remains for us to live as though it were not so. But to me the future is still black and blank – is a vast ignorance, lit at a few casual places by the memory of his story.[3] And I have by me, for my comfort, two strange white flowers – shrivelled now, and brown and flat and brittle – to witness that even when mind and strength had gone, gratitude and a mutual tenderness still lived on in the heart of man.

Appendix: Wells's Preface (1931)

The *Time Machine* was published in 1895. It is obviously the work of an inexperienced writer, but certain originalities in it saved it from extinction and there are still publishers and perhaps even readers to be found for it after the lapse of a third of a century. In its final form, except for certain minor amendments, it was written in a lodging at Sevenoaks in Kent. The writer was then living from hand to mouth as a journalist. There came a lean month when scarcely an article of his was published or paid for in any of the papers to which he was accustomed to contribute and since all the offices in London that would tolerate him were already amply supplied with still unused articles, it seemed hopeless to write more until the block moved. Accordingly, rather than fret at this dismaying change in his outlook, he wrote this story in the chance of finding a market for it in some new quarter. He remembers writing at it late one summer night by an open window, while a disagreeable landlady grumbled at him in the darkness outside because of the excessive use of her lamp, expanding to a dreaming world her unwillingness to go to bed while that lamp was still alight; he wrote on to that accompaniment; and he remembers, too, discussing it and the underlying notions of it, while he walked in Knole Park with that dear companion who sustained him so stoutly through those adventurous years of short commons and hopeful uncertainty.

The idea of it seemed in those days to be his 'one idea'. He had saved it up so far in the hope that he would one day make a much longer book of it than the *Time Machine*, but the urgent need for something marketable obliged him to exploit it forthwith. As the discerning reader will perceive, it is a very unequal book: the early discussion is much more carefully planned and written than the later chapters. A slender story springs from a very profound root. The early part, the explanation of the idea had already seen the light in 1893 in Henley's *National Observer*.[1] It was the latter half that was written so urgently at Sevenoaks in 1894.

That one idea is now everybody's idea. It was never the writer's own peculiar idea. Other people were coming to it. It was begotten in the writer's mind by students' discussions in the laboratories and debating society of the Royal College of Science in the eighties and already it had been tried over in various forms by him before he made this particular application of it. It is the idea that Time is a fourth dimension and that the normal present is a three-dimensional section of a four-dimensional universe. The only difference between the time dimension and the others, from this point of view, lay in the movement of consciousness along it, whereby the progress of the present was constituted. Obviously there might be various 'presents' according to the direction in which the advancing section was cut, a method of stating the conception of relativity that did not come into scientific use until a considerable time later, and as obviously, since the section called the 'present' was real and not 'mathematical', it would possess a certain depth that might vary. The 'now' therefore is not instantaneous, it is a shorter or longer measure of time, a point that has still to find its proper appreciation in contemporary thought.

But my story does not go on to explore either of these possibilities; I did not in the least know how to go on to such an exploration. I was not sufficiently educated in that field, and certainly a story was not the way to investigate further. So my opening exposition escapes along the line of paradox to an imaginative romance stamped with many characteristics of the Stevenson and early-Kipling period in which it was written. Already the writer had made an earlier experiment in the pseudo-Teutonic, Nathaniel Hawthorne style, an experiment printed in the *Science Schools Journal* (1888–89) and now happily unattainable.[2] All the gold of Mr Gabriel Wells[3] cannot recover that version. And there was also an account of the idea, set up to be printed for the *Fortnightly Review* in 1891 and never used. It was there called 'The Universe Rigid'. That too is lost beyond recovery, though a less unorthodox predecessor 'The Rediscovery of the Unique', insisting upon the individuality of atoms, saw the light in the July issue of that year. Then the editor Mr Frank Harris woke up to the fact that he was printing matter twenty years too soon, reproached the writer terrifyingly, and broke type again. If any impression survives it must be in the archives of the *Fortnightly Review* but I doubt if any impression survives. For years I thought I had a copy but when I looked for it, it had gone.

The story of the *Time Machine* as distinguished from the idea, 'dates' not only in its treatment but in its conception. It seems a very undergraduate performance to its now mature writer, as he looks it over once more. But it goes as far as his philosophy about human evolution went in those days. The idea of a social differentiation of mankind into Eloi and Morlocks, strikes him now as more than a little crude. In his adolescence Swift had exercised a tremendous fascination upon him and the naive pessimism of this picture of the human future is, like the kindred *Island of Doctor Moreau*, a clumsy tribute to a master to whom he owes an enormous debt. Moreover, the geologists and astronomers of that time told us dreadful lies about the 'inevitable' freezing up of the world – and of life and mankind with it. There was no escape it seemed. The whole game of life would be over in a million years or less. They impressed this upon us with the full weight of their authority, while now Sir James Jeans[4] in his smiling *Universe Around Us* waves us on to millions of millions of years. Given as much law as that man will be able to do anything and go anywhere, and the only trace of pessimism left in the human prospect today is a faint flavour of regret that one was born so soon. And even from that distress modern psychological and biological philosophy offers ways of escape.

One must err to grow and the writer feels no remorse for this youthful effort. Indeed he hugs his vanity very pleasantly at times when his dear old *Time Machine* crops up once more in essays and speeches, still a practical and convenient way to retrospect or prophecy. *The Time Journey of Doctor Barton,*[5] dated 1929, is upon his desk as he writes – with all sorts of things in it we never dreamt of six and thirty years ago. So the *Time Machine* has lasted as long as the diamond-framed safety bicycle, which came in at about the date of its first publication. And now it is going to be printed and published so admirably that its author is assured it will outlive him. He has long since given up the practice of writing prefaces for books, but this is an exceptional occasion and he is very proud and happy to say a word or so of reminiscence and friendly commendation for that needy and cheerful namesake of his, who lived back along the time dimension, six and thirty years ago.

H. G. WELLS

NOTES

1. *The early part, the explanation of the idea had already seen the light in 1893 in Henley's National Observer*: Wells mistakes the date of an early version of *The Time Machine* in this instance. A series of seven linked articles, commissioned by William Ernest Henley and entitled 'The Time Traveller's Story', was in fact serialized in the *National Observer* between March and June 1894.

2. *Already the writer had made an earlier experiment ... now happily unattainable*: Wells is referring to 'The Chronic Argonauts', a short story published in the *Science Schools Journal* between April and June 1888, in which he first introduced the concept of a time machine.

3. *Mr Gabriel Wells*: A wealthy American book dealer.

4. *Sir James Jeans*: *The Universe Around Us* was published in 1929. Jeans (1877–1946) was the author of a number of popular works on astronomy and physics in the 1920s and 1930s. His other works included *Through Space and Time* (1934).

5. *The Time Journey of Doctor Barton*: Was subtitled *An Engineering and Sociological Forecast Based on Present Possibilities*, edited by John Hodgson.

Notes

SECTION 1

1. *Professor Simon Newcomb was expounding this to the New York Mathematical Society only a month or so ago*: Simon Newcomb (1835–1909) spoke on the possibility of constructing a four-dimensional geometry at a meeting of the New York Mathematical Society in December 1893. Wells was probably familiar with 'Modern Mathematical Thought', a transcription of Newcomb's address published in *Nature*, 49 (1 February 1894), pp. 325–9. This reference to Newcomb provides a valuable clue in determining the probable date of the Time Traveller's dinner party. The Medical Man's recollection of 'that ghost you showed us last Christmas' (p. 11) may well be taken to imply that the Traveller's guests visit his house around December 1893.
2. *Battle of Hastings*: An engagement fought on 14 October 1066 near Hastings by King Harold II of England against the invasion of William, Duke of Normandy. The Norman victory and death of Harold marked the end of the Anglo-Saxon monarchy and produced a social revolution.
3. *plough you for the Little-go*: Fail you for the preliminary examination, taken at Oxford and Cambridge universities.
4. *Burslem*: One of the six towns that aggregate to form Stoke-on-Trent, in the English Midlands.

SECTION 2

1. *Linnaean*: Learned society, founded in 1788, at a meeting of which Charles Darwin and Alfred Russel Wallace jointly announced the theory of natural selection on 1 July 1858.
2. *Tübingen*: A German university town.
3. *Richmond*: A residential suburb on the River Thames about 9

miles south-west of central London. The Wandsworth area of London mentioned by the Traveller (p. 64) is about 4 miles to the east of Richmond, while Battersea is approximately 6 miles east of Richmond. The Banstead site of the Palace of Green Porcelain (p. 52) is about 18 miles south of Richmond.

4. *been doing the Amateur Cadger*: Posing as a beggar.

5. *eke out his modest income with a crossing? or has he his Nebuch-adnezzar phases*: The Editor poses two guesses in an attempt to explain the Time Traveller's dishevelled appearance. He first asks whether the protagonist works as a street sweeper. Secondly he wonders whether, like King Nebuchadnezzar after losing his throne, the Time Traveller has been forced to live with the wild animals (see Daniel 4:28–33).

6. *the new kind of journalist – very joyous, irreverent young men*: Probably a reference to the New Journalism, characterized by sensationalist, investigative reporting and pioneered by William Thomas Stead (1849–1912).

7. *little Rosebery*: The Editor is obviously hoping to ascertain the future outcome of some impending event. This event might be linked with the political fate of the Earl of Rosebery, who became British prime minister in 1894 following Gladstone's resignation as leader of the Liberal party. This reference to 'little Rosebery' was not present in the early version of *The Time Machine* serialized in the *National Observer*. Its inclusion in the final version of *The Time Machine* published in book form on 29 May 1895 could be a response to the imminent election of June 1895.

8. *peptone*: Protein.

9. *a shilling a line for a verbatim note*: The Editor is again attempting to profit from a knowledge of the future, since he hopes to scoop an exclusive story.

10. *Hettie Potter*: Unidentified. The context suggests that Potter was some sort of popular entertainer, possibly a contemporary actress or music hall singer.

SECTION 3

1. *in shape something like a winged sphinx*: In Greek mythology, the sphinx was the winged monster of Thebes, with the head of a woman and the body of a lion. The term sphinx also refers to any of several ancient Egyptian stone carvings having a lion's body and a human or animal head.

SECTION 4

1. *I fancied I saw suggestions of old Phoenician decorations*: Phoenician culture played an important role in establishing the foundations of Western civilization. The Phoenicians were thought to have introduced the alphabet to the Greeks, for example. With this reference to Phoenician culture, Wells may have intended to critique the British Empire by contrasting its relative historical insignificance with the enduring influence of classical culture.

2. *Ichthyosaurus*: A fossil marine reptile of the Mesozoic era, resembling a dolphin with a long pointed head, four flippers and a vertical tail.

3. *specialization of the sexes*: In the 1890s, there was a perception that specialized gender roles were already disappearing. Wells himself later advocated a degree of specialization between the sexes in his proposed endowment of motherhood scheme of the 1900s. Wells argued that making regular state payments to mothers dependent upon the satisfactory progress of the child would provide a woman with economic independence from her husband and, more importantly, ensure the well-being of future generations.

SECTION 5

1. *the full moon ... gibbous*: The moon is in its 'gibbous' phase when it is between half and full. The implication in this passage is that the moon is actually approaching full, since it cannot be both gibbous and full at the same time.

2. *monomania*: A psychological disorder, discussed throughout the nineteenth century, in which an individual becomes preoccupied with a single interest or idea.

3. *Weena*: It has been suggested that Wells derived the name Weena from Zee, the heroine of Edward Bulwer Lytton's utopian novel, *The Coming Race*.

4. *a queer notion of Grant Allen's*: Grant Allen (1848–99) was a novelist, essayist, advocate of evolutionary theory and social reformer. He was also a friend and correspondent of Wells. The story being alluded to in this instance is 'Pallinghurst Barrow' (1892).

5. *the younger Darwin ... the planets must ultimately fall back one*

by one into the parent body: A reference to the work of George Howard Darwin, the son of the naturalist Charles Darwin and an eminent astronomer. Darwin (1845–1912) theorized that the distance between the moon and earth was affected by 'tidal friction', which was responsible for the speed of the earth's rotation. He argued that the moon had originally broken away from the earth; once it had reached a maximum distance, it would begin to draw near again. Darwin initially argued that his 'tidal friction' theory could explain the evolution of the entire solar system, although he subsequently discarded this view.

6.   *Lemur*: Lemur refers both to a family of prosimian mammals, and to a ghost or spirit of the dead.

7.   *there is the Metropolitan Railway in London*: The London Underground, which formed part of the Metropolitan Railway, was first opened in 1863.

8.   *Even now, does not an East-end worker live in such artificial conditions as practically to be cut off from the natural surface of the earth*: The plight of the poor was a significant social concern of the 1880s and 1890s. Figures like William Booth and Andrew Mearns investigated living conditions in the East End of London, and found, among other deficiencies, that the homes of the poor were not receiving adequate light or fresh air.

9.   *that exchange between class and class . . . less and less frequent*: Probably a sardonic reference to Francis Galton's notion of 'positive' eugenics. In a number of works beginning with the publication of *Inquiries into Human Faculty and its Development* (1883), Galton campaigned for the public endowment of marriages between gifted couples from eminent British families ('positive' eugenics). Galton argued that, since the offspring of two gifted individuals is more likely to possess such desirable qualities as energy and intelligence, positive eugenics is the most productive way of increasing the 'favoured stock' of a nation. Wells in *The Time Machine* expresses his view that, rather than increasing the productivity of the 'favoured stock', endowing marriages between members of the privileged classes would simply result in the type of division of humanity signified in the evolutionary opposition between the Eloi and the Morlocks.

10. *I had no convenient cicerone in the pattern of the Utopian books*: A cicerone is a tourist guide. In most late-nineteenth-century utopian novels, a guide shows the visitor around the good society. In the *National Observer* version of *The Time Machine*, Wells is explicitly scornful of this convention. William Morris's *News*

From Nowhere (1890) was probably uppermost in his mind when he wrote that:

> Odd as it may seem, I had no cicerone. In all the narratives of people visiting the future that I have read, some obliging scandal-monger appears at an early stage, and begins to lecture on constitutional history and social economy, and to point out the celebrities. Indeed so little had I thought of the absurdity of this that I had actually anticipated something of the kind would occur in reality. (H. G. Wells, 'The Refinement of Humanity', *National Observer* 11 (21 April 1894), p. 581)

11. *The too-perfect security of the Upperworlders had led them to a slow movement of degeneration, to a general dwindling in size, strength and intelligence*: Throughout his life, Wells emphasized his indebtedness to T. H. Huxley, who taught him in his first year of study at the Normal School of Science (1884–7). In 'The Struggle for Existence in Human Society' (1888), Huxley challenged the popular consensus that evolution would inevitably lead to increased perfection of mankind. By making the 'general dwindling in size, strength and intelligence' among the Eloi a consequence of the 'too perfect security' of their environment, Wells applies the Huxleian principle of 'retrogressive metamorphosis' to humanity in *The Time Machine*.

12. *Morlocks . . . Eloi*: Morlock and Eloi are both names of probable biblical origin. The name Morlock appears to have been derived from the biblical 'Moloch' or 'Molech'. According to Jeremiah 7:31 an altar was built to Moloch near Jerusalem even though passing sons and daughters through fire was forbidden according to the law laid down by Moses (Deuteronomy 18:10). The origin of the name Eloi is the moment when Jesus questions God on the cross: '*Eloi, Eloi, lama sabachthani?*' (Matthew 27:47–8).

SECTION 6

1. *halitus*: A vapour, an exhalation.
2. *Kodak*: The first portable Kodak camera was marketed in 1890.

SECTION 7

1. *Carlovingian kings*: The ninth-century successors to the Frankish kingdom founded by Charlemagne.

2. *Sirius*: Part of the constellation Canis Major (the 'big dog'), Sirius (the 'dog' star) is the brightest star in the sky.
3. *one bright planet*: Probably Venus.
4. *the great precessional cycle . . . Only forty times*: The precessional cycle is the rotation of the pole of the equator round the pole of the ecliptic. Each cycle takes approximately 25,800 years to complete. In the time across which the Traveller's machine has leapt, it should in fact have occurred just over thirty-one times.
5. *Carlyle-like scorn of this wretched aristocracy in decay*: Thomas Carlyle was a Scottish historian and political philosopher (1795–1881). In Book 3, Ch. 8 of *Past and Present* (1843), Carlyle foresees the demise of the 'Idle Aristocracy, the Owners of the soil of England', for whom 'a thinking eye discerns ghastly images of ruin, too ghastly for words'.

SECTION 8

1. *Megatherium*: An extinct giant sloth from South America.
2. *Brontosaurus*: Another term for apatosaurus, a huge herbivorous dinosaur of the late Jurassic period, with a long neck and tail. There is a degree of unconscious irony in the protagonist recalling a herbivorous animal here, since he discovers that the carnivorous Morlocks are feeding on the Eloi.
3. *the ruins of some latter-day South Kensington*: A reference to the South Kensington Museum, which in the Victorian era was an umbrella term for the museums of arts and science established with the proceeds from the Great Exhibition of 1851. They now form four separate institutions: the Geological Museum, the Natural History Museum, the Science Museum and the Victoria and Albert Museum.
4. *Philosophical Transactions*: The journal of the Royal Society, begun in 1665 by Henry Oldenburg.
5. *The Land of the Leal*: A Scots ballad.
6. *Belemnite*: An extinct cephalopod or mollusc.

SECTION 9

1. *carbuncles*: A carbuncle is a bright red gem.

SECTION 10

1. *It is a law of nature we overlook . . . Only those animals partake
    of intelligence that have to meet a huge variety of needs and
    dangers*: Wells's source here was undoubtedly Edwin Ray Lanke-
    ster's *Degeneration: A Chapter in Darwinism*. Lankester identi-
    fied the parasite as a long-recognized instance of degeneration,
    which is subject to what he terms *retrogressive metamorphosis*.
    Since its food and safety are very easily attained, the parasitic
    animal gradually loses its capacity to adapt. Rather like the
    parasitic animal described by Lankester, the Eloi race has lost its
    capacity to adapt as a consequence of its food and safety having
    been easily attained. Lankester's notion of *retrogressive meta-
    morphosis* probably also influenced Wells's essay 'Zoological
    Retrogression' (1891).

SECTION 11

1. *the work of the tidal drag was done*: A second reference to G. H.
    Darwin's theory of the 'tidal drag'. Wells assumes that tidal drag
    affects the whole solar system. (See also Section 5, note 5.)
2. *salt Dead Sea*: An enclosed area of water, 46 miles long and up
    to 10 miles broad with high salt content, into which the River
    Jordan debouches. Fish cannot swim in it (cf. Ezek. 47:9, 10).
    Wells extrapolates from the absence of marine life in this sea in
    order to emphasize the almost lifeless desolation of the earth in
    the remote future.

SECTION 12

1. *Hillyer*: It has been suggested that Hillyer is the narrator. Assum-
    ing this to be the case, this moment probably corresponds to the
    point where the narrator sees the Time Traveller as 'a ghostly,
    indistinct figure sitting in a whirling mass of black and brass for
    a moment' (p. 90).
2. *Pall Mall Gazette*: A London-based journal to which Wells was
    a frequent contributor between 1893 and 1895. As well as his
    literary reviews, the *Pall Mall Gazette* published some of Wells's
    scientific journalism, notably 'The Man of the Year Million'
    (1893).
3. *overwork*: Contemporary medical science emphasized the

importance of conserving nervous energy to mental welfare. Excessive overwork was thought to induce a drain of nervous energy. Physical symptoms included paleness of the complexion, which explains why the Medical Man 'looked into' the Time Traveller's face before telling him that he was suffering from overwork.

EPILOGUE

1. *plesiosaurus*: A large fossil marine reptile of the Mesozoic era, with large paddlelike limbs and a long flexible neck.
2. *Oolitic*: Of or relating to limestone consisting of a mass of rounded grains (ooliths) made up of concentric layers.
3. *But to me the future is still black and blank – is a vast ignorance, lit at a few casual places by the memory of his story*: The narrator's comment here recalls an important passage from 'The Rediscovery of the Unique' (1891), in which Wells stresses the potential of scientific knowledge to reveal the comparative insignificance of humanity in the cosmic order:

> Science is a match that man has just got alight. He thought he was in a room – in moments of devotion, a temple – and that his light would be reflected from and display walls inscribed with wonderful secrets and pillars carved with philosophical systems wrought into harmony. It is a curious sensation, now that the preliminary splutter is over and the flame burns up clear, to see his hands lit and just a glimpse of himself and the patch he stands on visible, and around him, in place of all that human comfort and beauty he anticipated – darkness still. (H. G. Wells, 'The Rediscovery of the Unique', *Fortnightly Review* n.s. 50 (1891), p. 111)

PENGUIN CLASSICS

THE HISTORY OF MR POLLY H. G. WELLS

'He had a curious feeling that it would be very satisfying to marry and have a wife – only somehow he wished it wasn't Miriam'

Mr Polly is an ordinary middle-aged man who is tired of his wife's nagging and his dreary job as the owner of a regional gentleman's outfitters. Faced with the threat of bankruptcy, he concludes that the only way to escape his frustrating existence is by burning his shop to the ground, and killing himself. Unexpected events, however, conspire at the last moment to lead the bewildered Mr Polly to a bright new future – after he saves a life, fakes his death, and escapes to a life of heroism, hope and ultimate happiness.

Widely regarded as Wells's funniest novel, *The History of Mr Polly* is a compelling account of one man's triumph against social obligation. Part of a brand new Penguin series of H. G. Wells's works, this edition includes a newly-established text, a full biographical essay on Wells, a further reading list and detailed notes. In his introduction John Sutherland considers the character of Mr Polly and his relevance to Wells's own life.

Introduced by John Sutherland

Textual Editing by Simon J. James

Notes by John Sutherland and Simon J. James

THE STORY OF PENGUIN CLASSICS

Before 1946 ...'Classics' are mainly the domain of academics and students, without readable editions for everyone else. This all changes when a little-known classicist, E. V. Rieu, presents Penguin founder Allen Lane with the translation of Homer's *Odyssey* that he has been working on and reading to his wife Nelly in his spare time.

1946 *The Odyssey* becomes the first Penguin Classic published, and promptly sells three million copies. Suddenly, classic books are no longer for the privileged few.

1950s Rieu, now series editor, turns to professional writers for the best modern, readable translations, including Dorothy L. Sayers's *Inferno* and Robert Graves's *The Twelve Caesars*, which revives the salacious original.

1960s The Classics are given the distinctive black jackets that have remained a constant throughout the series's various looks. Rieu retires in 1964, hailing the Penguin Classics list as 'the greatest educative force of the 20th century'.

1970s A new generation of translators arrives to swell the Penguin Classics ranks, and the list grows to encompass more philosophy, religion, science, history and politics.

1980s The Penguin American Library joins the Classics stable, with titles such as *The Last of the Mohicans* safeguarded. Penguin Classics now offers the most comprehensive library of world literature available.

1990s The launch of Penguin Audiobooks brings the classics to a listening audience for the first time, and in 1999 the launch of the Penguin Classics website takes them online to a larger global readership than ever before.

The 21st Century Penguin Classics are rejacketed for the first time in nearly twenty years. This world famous series now consists of more than 1300 titles, making the widest range of the best books ever written available to millions – and constantly redefining the meaning of what makes a 'classic'.

The Odyssey continues ...

The best books ever written

PENGUIN (Ⓟ) CLASSICS

SINCE 1946

Find out more at www.penguinclassics.com